Matt tugged on the clipboard.
"What's that?"

Kerry looked down in dismay. During her daydreaming her hands had taken over and sketched his face.

"Oh, that," she said, forcing a grin. "I saw the dartboard in the game room and thought it needed a new target."

"Very funny." He tried to glare, but the slight curve of his mouth gave him away. "That works both ways, you know."

He leaned closer, smiling, and she pressed against the ticket counter behind her. "W-what do you mean, 'works both ways'?"

"If you make me a target, I can also set my sights on you."

Dear Reader,

If you're at all like me, you enjoy books that have a special connection to your own life, whether it's through a heroine's occupation, a setting in a place you once visited, or a character who is dealing with a tough situation you've had to handle, too.

Family Matters is special to me in many ways.

I love the knight-in-mirrored-sunglasses hero, the conflicted but committed heroine and the quirky townsfolk who play key roles all through the story.

I also love the setting, which creates a whole list of problems in the book. Don't blame me! The characters wanted to buy their own amusement park, and how could I turn them down?

Most of all—and where *Family Matters* really hits home for me—I love that the heroine comes from an Irish family, which ties in to my own Irish roots. Kerry's family is one of a kind, though. It's large. It's crazy. And it's filled with a bunch of eccentrics you'll soon get to meet.

I hope you have as much fun reading this book as I did writing it! Feel free to drop me a note and let me know. You can reach me at P.O. Box 504, Gilbert, AZ 85299 or through my Web site, www.barbarawhitedaille.com.

All my best to you!

Until we meet again,

Barbara White Daille

Family Matters

BARBARA WHITE DAILLE

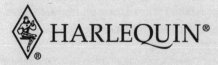

TORONTO • NEW YORK • LONDON
AMSTERDAM • PARIS • SYDNEY • HAMBURG
STOCKHOLM • ATHENS • TOKYO • MILAN • MADRID
PRAGUE • WARSAW • BUDAPEST • AUCKLAND

Recycling programs
for this product may
not exist in your area.

ISBN-13: 978-0-373-75332-1

FAMILY MATTERS

ABOUT THE AUTHOR

When she was very young, Barbara White Daille learned from her mom about the storytelling magic in books—and she's been hooked ever since. Now thrilled to be an author herself, she hopes you will enjoy reading her books and will find your own magic in them! Originally from the East Coast, Barbara lives with her husband in the warm, sunny Southwest, where they love the dry heat and have taken up square-dancing.

Books by Barbara White Daille

HARLEQUIN AMERICAN ROMANCE
1131—THE SHERIFF'S SON
1140—COURT ME, COWBOY

In memory of Dolores F. White,
for giving me both the love
of reading and my Irish roots

And, as always, to Rich

Many thanks to Johanna Raisanen
for her keen eye and thought-provoking comments

Chapter One

As always, willing or not, Kerry MacBride came soaring to the rescue. When her final paycheck for the school year arrived, she really should splurge on a pair of bright tights and a cape.

Heart thumping in time with her sprinting footsteps, she rushed down the all-too-familiar main hallway of Lakeside Village's clubhouse, the center of this age-fifty-plus planned community and, in fact, the social hub of the entire town.

As if the future residents of the community had planned it that way—and knowing Gran and some of the other residents, they probably had—the Village sat smack in the middle of her tiny hometown of Lakeside, Illinois. From various vantage points on the property, you could look in all directions and see just about everything worth seeing.

Right now, all *she* wanted to see was both Gran and Uncle Bren safe inside the facility's game room, where the volunteer at the front desk had told her she would find them.

She had her doubts, though. Who wouldn't, after the message she'd heard on her voice mail earlier that afternoon?

Well, Kerry, Uncle Bren had rumbled into her ear in farewell, *the next time you see me, it might be behind bars.*

She should know better than to fall for this. Or to get involved in another one of his crazy schemes. Or even to drop everything—on a Thursday, no less—and head for home on the off chance he was telling the truth.

With one more day of school left, she hadn't planned to come down until the weekend. She should be home right now, packing for her dream-of-a-lifetime trip. She, who had never left Illinois, would be spending the summer in Europe! It still dumbfounded her to realize she had been chosen for the art fellowship.

But, though the plea went unspoken, she'd heard the desperation beneath Uncle Bren's words. That fact had her making the drive from her apartment in Chicago to Lakeside in less than three hours. Under the speed limit, too, of course. Barely.

Kerry also knew better than to risk a run-in with a police officer. But Uncle Bren? And Gran? Much as she loved them both, it wouldn't surprise her to find either of them in trouble.

She burst through the doorway into the game room, skidded to a halt on the polished tile floor, and confronted chaos.

The room overflowed with people, all yelling at once. The loudest roar came from a dark-haired man tall enough to dwarf Uncle Bren's near-six-foot frame. The man, slim but muscular in a pearl-gray suit, looked ready to split the jacket's seams with his wide-armed gestures.

Thank goodness, Gran stood safely out of his reach. But Uncle Bren, hemmed in by the crowd, faced the brunt of the stranger's anger.

Even without her years of artistic training, Kerry would have seen something wrong with this picture.

"Excuse me," she said, using her project-to-the-back-of-the-classroom tone. "What do you think you're doing?" The question drowned out every voice in the room. The shouting subsided and every head turned her way.

As she moved forward, people parted, allowing her to pass.

A slim older woman stood beside the man confronting Uncle Bren. She put her hand on his arm. "Matthew, sweetheart—"

"It's all right, Mom, I'll handle this."

As Kerry approached, the woman glanced at her, frowned anxiously in Bren's direction, then took what looked like a reluctant step back.

The man now faced Kerry, his eyes dark with anger. She caught her breath at the fury in his expression but didn't break stride until she'd reached him.

Looking up—way up—she met his gaze. "What's going on here?"

After a long, tense silence, he answered, his tone level. "We're holding a meeting."

She widened her eyes. "It sounded to me more like you're having an argument."

Behind him, Uncle Bren stood unmoving but nodded in confirmation. Trust him to let her pick up the problem and run with it.

The man took a deep breath, which now strained the buttons on his immaculate white shirt, and traced his thumbnail across one eyebrow. "I only argue before a jury. As we're not in court—*yet*—that doesn't apply here."

She swallowed a wave of panic. "You're a lawyer?"

"Yes."

Great. A lawyer who had just stood ranting at Uncle Bren. Things couldn't get any worse. Or could they? And did she really want to know? "You look like you could use a little assistance with this…meeting."

He smiled. Despite the situation, she couldn't help but notice how it changed his entire expression, easing the hard frown lines bisecting his forehead, even lightening the color of his eyes from near black to a dark greenish-gray. An interesting transformation.

She didn't trust the change in him for a minute.

Still, she squinted at him and found her head tilting slightly, her fingers curling around an imaginary paintbrush. With an effort, she blinked, bringing herself back to harsh reality.

"I could use a warrant and a padded cell." He gestured over his shoulder. "If you think you've got any chance of knocking some sense into that scam artist, go right ahead."

She squinted again, not in pleasure this time. "Wait a minute—"

"You've got no call to say that," Uncle Bren interrupted, glaring at the man.

He sounded intimidating enough, but Kerry knew the real threat would come from her grandmother, always famous for jumping into any brawl.

Kerry looked over her shoulder. Sure enough, here Gran came, pushing her way through the crowd, barreling toward the lawyer and Uncle Bren. Kerry moved hastily toward her. Fortunately, as she closed in, the crowd surged around them both.

"Out of my way, Kerry Anne. I don't let anyone use such talk to my family, children nor grandchildren." She added ominously, "And you know what happens when I get my Irish up."

"I *do* know, Gran," Kerry agreed.

"Maeve, we need you here," one of the residents called.

Gran started pushing again, heading in that direction. Kerry breathed a sigh of relief but couldn't help looking fondly after her.

Kerry had spent most of her childhood living down what happened when Gran's temper got the better of her—though, she had to admit, the results were sometimes all to the good. Such as the time Mom and Dad, both archaeologists, had wanted to leave their offspring permanently with Gran and Grandpa to head off for parts unknown. Children weren't allowed to spend more than brief visits at Lakeside Village, but Gran had fixed that.

The story Gran told about taking on the raising of her grandkids had been repeated so often, it now had the flavor of family legend.

The nerve of them, trying to keep my grandchildren out of the Village and my own home, too. At that point, Gran would smile wickedly and add, *All it took was me getting my Irish up—and threatening to share more local scandals than you'll ever see on those daytime television shows.*

Kerry didn't doubt Gran would have done it, too, if necessary. Luckily, everything had worked out, and she and her brothers had grown up with Gran and Grandpa—with occasional long visits from Uncle Bren.

Thinking of him and this situation made Kerry sigh.

The crowed shifted, buffeting her aside. Reluctantly, she turned back to the lawyer and found him standing in front of her.

Glowering, they stared each other down.

Before Kerry could speak, a deep voice called out, "All right, now, folks, let's settle down and regroup."

She recognized Albie Gardner, leader of the residents' association, on the fringe of the crowd. He stood wider than he was tall, his bare scalp just visible to her above the heads of the people between them. Albie's baritone cut through the high pitch of emotional outrage even more effectively than she had done.

"Matt Lawrence," he bellowed, "you called this meeting to order—not that we've seen a lot of orderliness around here yet. But it's only fair you get a chance to speak. You were gearing up to state an opinion."

"I was," the lawyer said emphatically.

When Matt turned away, Kerry took the opportunity to slip around him and stand closer to Uncle Bren.

"You've all got to see a project like this one is risky at best," Matt told them. "At worst, it's doomed from the start."

A pulse ticked in warning at Kerry's temple. *Something* had to account for an extreme statement like that one. And much as she hated to admit it, she could hear the concern beneath Matt Lawrence's words.

"You can't know how things'll end up," a woman called out.

"I can make a good assumption, though, based on how they began. Did you do any market research before you made your decision? Did MacBride show you any safety reports on the property? Or any kind of paperwork at all?"

The pulse in Kerry's head started banging away like the fire alarm bell in her classroom at school. *What* had Uncle Bren gotten these poor people into?

A woman across from their tight circle shook her head. "He's Maeve's son—he wouldn't steer us wrong."

"You're right about that," Gran put in smugly.

"Is that so?"

Matt's glare would have pinned Uncle Bren in place—if he'd noticed. Kerry couldn't miss it. Forget a trial and sentencing and time off for good behavior. This lawyer wanted a lynching. And it looked as if he wanted it now.

Almost unconsciously, Kerry took her uncle's arm.

"What's going to happen if the project never gets off the ground?" Matt pressed.

A few of the people around them shifted position, their faces crumpling into worry lines.

"It will," someone from the back of the room called.

Other voices chimed in.

"That's right."

"We'll see to it."

"Things will be fine."

"And if they're not?" Matt persisted. "Your investments will be gone."

"He does have a point," one trembling voice said.

Someone added agreement.

As the shouting rose again, Kerry felt her uncle jump. She shot him a glance and leaned close to whisper, "What's this all about, Uncle Bren?"

She could feel him stiffen, sense his reluctance to speak. Trying to force the words through her suddenly tight throat, she repeated, "Uncle Bren?"

"Well," he whispered, "I—I've up and bought Rainbow's End."

"You've *what?*" Shock made her speak out loud, but with all the commotion around them, no one noticed. Except Matt Lawrence, who narrowed his eyes and focused on her mouth as if wanting to read her lips. A tremor of dismay rippled through her.

Turning sideways to block Matt's view, she blurted, "Uncle Bren, are you…?" Biting off the words with an effort, she felt helpless to do anything but shake her head at him.

He looked crestfallen—for all of three seconds. Then he rallied, announcing with the usual Brendan MacBride aplomb, "Kerry, me girl, it was a steal."

She prayed he didn't mean those words literally. Already, the news was more than she could bear. How could *anyone* have supported Uncle Bren in buying a derelict amusement park? All of Lakeside knew he belonged to the eccentric MacBride clan. Yet, if what Matt Lawrence had said was true, her uncle had persuaded this roomful of people—many of them retirees on limited incomes—to invest their savings in his wild idea.

"Uncle Bren," she said fiercely, knowing the uproar around them drowned out her voice, "you've got to give them their money back."

"I haven't got it," he admitted.

Swallowing a groan of frustration, she brought her trembling hand to her mouth. Uncle Bren had gotten into scrapes on a regular basis, for as far back as she could remember. They were always harmless, well-intentioned ideas that just hadn't worked out. They'd never involved anything on a scale like this. He'd really let himself in for trouble now.

Which meant Kerry was in trouble, too.

She had to stall. Had to buy *Uncle Bren* some time so *she* could find out what had happened to the money and figure out how to get him out of this predicament. She couldn't question him here, with that angry lawyer still watching.

As Albie joined their inner circle, the voices around them hushed. "I'm sure Bren has answers to all our concerns," he said to the crowd.

"Of course," Uncle Bren replied glibly.

Of course not, she would bet. But on the off chance he might be able to give her something to fight with, she grabbed at his words.

"Yes, he has answers," she announced firmly, focusing on Albie and trying not to notice Matt's narrow-eyed glare. "He'll just need some time to pull them together."

Matt made a choking sound indicating disbelief. She ignored that, too.

"Seems reasonable," Albie said. "Bren, why don't you take the next couple of days and come up with a proposal that will address everyone's concerns."

"Hold on," Matt said. "If he didn't have all the answers up front, what was he doing signing a contract?"

"I'm sure we'll find out. Bren, give us a rough idea of where we stand with the project. And where we're going with it."

"Not a problem." Uncle Bren grinned.

"Not at all," Kerry confirmed. What choice did she have? The plane for Europe took off in a week. She was going to be on it. You didn't give up the chance of a lifetime…second time around. Right after college graduation, she'd received a fellowship offer, too—and another family disaster had upset all her plans. That wouldn't happen now.

A week gave her plenty of time to save Uncle Bren.

"What makes you qualified to draw up a business plan?" Matt Lawrence asked him.

"Me," she said flatly, before Uncle Bren could reply.

Matt turned her way. "You?"

She nodded. "I've taken business and art management classes and spent a summer supervising an art festival in Chicago. Outlining a game plan for an amusement park will be a snap."

Matt locked gazes with her. His eyes, now dark again, generated enough heat to make her flush—outside *and* in. Even so, she stood unblinking, unable to force herself to look away. Frozen in place, like Bambi trapped by the headlights of an oncoming 18-wheeler.

OVER HER SHOULDER, Kerry watched Albie lead Matt Lawrence from the room. Matt continued talking, fast and furiously, even as they went through the doorway into the hall. He hadn't been at all happy about Uncle Bren's reprieve.

The rest of the group disbanded, leaving the game room quickly and a lot more quietly than Matt had done. Somehow, Gran had slipped away with them, too.

Fine with Kerry. She needed time alone with Uncle Bren, a chance to get the full story, without anyone—especially that lawyer—in their vicinity.

Sighing in relief, she turned back to her wayward relative, put her hands on her hips and looked up at him.

"Well, it's grand to see you," he said hurriedly, in an obvious attempt at nonchalance that didn't fool her one bit. "But

I thought you were still wrapping things up at that school of yours. What brings you here?"

"What…?" Struggling to snap her mouth shut, she focused on the rack of pool cues on the wall beside them. By the time she'd counted every last one, she could speak in a normal tone again. More or less.

"Tell me you're not serious, Uncle Bren. After the voice mail you left me? And then when I couldn't reach either you or Gran at the house and Gran didn't answer her cell phone…?"

"Nothing to worry about."

"Nothing?" That was the trouble with her uncle. Or the secret to his success. He could never see the error of his own ways. "No, nothing to concern me—only the thought of you being arrested for who knows what. Oh, Uncle Bren…"

She loved her family. Every last crazy one of them.

The stress of her frantic three-hour trip home, filled with worry about them, and then the shock of what had just taken place—all of it suddenly took its toll. Her despair must have shown in her shaking voice and slumping shoulders because he opened his arms wide to her.

She reached up, hugged him fiercely, then stepped back, the better to observe him. Even though he was nearing sixty, he looked the same as always, from as far back as her memory could take her. Broad-shouldered, dark-haired, with maybe a touch more silver now highlighting his temples, Maeve MacBride's eldest son made what her friends often called "a fine figure of a man." Bright blue eyes looked at her guilelessly, as if he hadn't a care in the world.

So typically Uncle Bren.

"Honestly, what were you thinking?" She shook her head. "The park has sat abandoned for years. Every single building on the pier is probably falling-down rotten. Please tell me— what in the world ever made you buy Rainbow's End?"

"I can do better than talk about it. I'll show you." He urged her toward the door.

Surrendering to the inevitable, she let him escort her from the room.

At the other end of the hallway, Matt stood near the management office talking emphatically to Albie Gardner. When he saw them, he cut himself off and stared. The look he sent their way gave her a chill, making her practically push Uncle Bren through the clubhouse's front doors.

Chapter Two

Kerry followed Uncle Bren outside into the fragrance and—to her—much-welcomed warmth of the mid-June afternoon. When he took her by the arm, she let him steer her toward the edge of a gentle grassy slope leading down to the lake that gave the town its name.

He swept his free hand majestically in the air and beamed, his unblinking gaze directed forward...until he looked from the corner of his eye and noticed she hadn't followed his lead. Raising his eyebrows, he gestured even more dramatically.

Sighing, she dragged her gaze across the sun-dappled water to the farside of the lake. There, a cluster of buildings sat on a small pier hugging the south shore. The sweeping curves of a roller coaster filled one end of the miniature boardwalk. The rounded frame of a Ferris wheel towered over it all.

The amusement park had closed down during her high school days and the rides had ceased running years before that. Still, the sight of Rainbow's End stirred many of her childhood memories. A great many of which she'd rather forget.

Swallowing hard, she did her best to hold back a groan. "What do you want with an old amusement park, anyhow? Did you even discuss this with Gran first?"

"Sure I did, and she's jumped on the deal with me—"

"No." This time, her groan escaped despite her effort to contain it. "Please tell me you didn't coerce her—"

"Kerry."

She tried to ignore his jaw-sagging expression of hurt. He was the man of a million faces, and who knew which ones you could trust?

"What do you take me for?" he went on. "Of course I didn't twist your gran's arm. Joining in was all her own idea." He grinned and added, "Besides, you know she won't do anything she doesn't have a mind to do."

"True enough." She tried a smile, feeling her face stretch like a newly framed canvas. "So. What exactly is your plan?"

"Rejuvenation!" he cried in the tones of a snake-oil salesman. "Revitalization! Resurrection! Put another way, we're going to bring Rainbow's End back to life."

"Not if that hotheaded lawyer kills it." The image of Matt's dark eyes was enough to make her shiver. This time, she wasn't sure why.

"Ah, now, Kerry, me girl, you'll not be doubting your uncle Brendan?"

The accentuated lilt in his voice gave him away. Gran always said Uncle Bren became more Irish than the Irish when he had something cooking. How could his own mother, knowing him so well, have fallen for his crazy scheme?

But of course, Gran was another unsteady branch on the MacBride family tree.

"It's all right," he continued. "That lad shook people up a bit just now, but I'd already won them over. Don't worry about a thing, Kerry—you know I kissed the Stone years ago."

She'd heard *that* bit of blarney before, with the previous idea. And all the ones before it. She swallowed the thoughts along with another gulp of air and asked, "What's the story with this lawyer?"

"Well, y'see…one of the ladies living here invested in the property with us—all her own doing, of course."

"Of course."

"And her son's giving her a hard time over it."

She thought of the tall woman who had hovered near the lawyer. The woman he'd called "Mom." "Not Matt Lawrence?" she asked without much hope.

"The very same." His sigh could have registered as a miniearthquake on the Richter scale. "He's got a bug up his britches about the whole deal. He positively insists he wants his ma's money returned. Obnoxious in manner he is about it, too—you saw him. But—" he rushed on before she could speak "—she advised we ignore the boy. Though that's hard to do when he's shown up on her doorstep."

"And when he's threatening you with legal action, if that's what your phone message meant." She crossed her arms and stared at him. "You've *got* to refund that one woman's money, at least, to get that attorney out of your hair."

"I can't."

"But—" Her tight throat made her choke on the words. "What happened to the money?"

"It's gone."

"You spent it *all* on that piece of…property over there?"

"Well, no. I wanted to get a jump on things, so I bought a few supplies, as well."

Luckily the tight throat held back her groan, too. "All right, it's not a major problem. You can return the supplies. And then you can see about selling the property, so you can return everyone's investment."

That earned her his guileless gaze once more. "What now, Uncle Bren?"

"Y'see…" He shrugged. "The owner drove a real hard bargain…"

"You're not telling me you paid more than market value?"

"Well, I didn't know at the time." He gave her a sheepish grin. "Besides, Rainbow's End is worth *any* amount of money to all of us here."

She closed her eyes, wishing that she had never woken up that morning. That she'd forgotten to charge her cell phone. That her parents had given her away at birth.

She couldn't wait to get an ocean away from here.

"The property could be a gold mine, Kerry."

Fool's gold, more than likely. But she didn't have the heart to say it aloud.

Just a few more days.... After closing up her classroom tomorrow, she would come back to Lakeside again for the weekend, whip Uncle Bren's proposal into shape and get him ready to take over this questionable enterprise.

Then she would go ahead with her own plans.

Opening her eyes, she looked at him and faked a reassuring smile.

He smiled back, tentatively at first, but then quickly recovered his normal happy-go-lucky grin. "It'll all work out, Kerry. That lawyer won't bother us again. You'll see."

All she could envision was the intensely bothersome Matt Lawrence as she'd seen him last, standing in the hallway with Albie and glaring at Kerry and Uncle Bren. Even the warm sunshine couldn't chase away the chill that sight had given her. This told her plainly their troubles with him weren't over yet.

In fact, they might just have begun.

WEARILY, MATT MOVED TOWARD the exit door of the clubhouse, his thoughts chaotic. He'd gotten nowhere with Albie Gardner, who insisted MacBride could have time to pull things together.

To Matt's way of thinking, that wasn't going to happen. But he was stymied now, stuck waiting for a couple of days before he could shoot down any cockeyed plan the man came up with. And Matt felt certain he could do it. He would have to.

He had to get his mom out of this mess.

She'd been taken in once before by a con man—the one she'd married. The one who had repaid his family's love by walking out on them.

The memory of his father storming out the door filled Matt with disgust. Still a child, he had sworn from that day forward he would protect his mother.

A promise he had spent all his adult life trying—and failing—to fulfill.

This time, he would succeed.

"Oh, Matthew."

The voice came unexpectedly from behind him, and he turned back. An older woman approached him, her step quick and sure. With her white hair, flowered dress and fluffy scarf, Maeve MacBride looked the picture of innocence. The perfect sweet old granny. Only she was the snake's mother, so how sweet and innocent could she be?

He tried to ignore the fact, attempted to think of her as any other elderly lady.

"Are you leaving us?" she asked, her lilting Irish brogue evidence of a childhood spent in the old country.

"Yes." They moved toward the exit. He held the door and escorted her out of the building. "But not right this minute." He'd just caught sight of MacBride across the walkway from the clubhouse. *Mom's so-called friend.* Beside him stood the cute redhead who'd defended the man during that fiasco of a meeting.

With mixed emotions, Matt moved forward.

Maeve sidestepped in front of him so abruptly he almost

crashed into her. Quickly, he rested a steadying hand on her arm. "What's wrong?"

"Just a touch of the sun." Her voice faltered. "Need a minute to get my old eyes adjusted."

He looked around. There was a sturdy wood and cast-iron bench conveniently placed just a few feet from the entrance doors. "Would you like to sit down?"

"Well, I…" She glanced toward her son and the redhead, then back at him. "No need. You can unhand me, laddie. All's well."

Matt followed her gaze. The redhead now stood alone. MacBride was long gone.

He snapped his gaze back to Maeve. Sure enough, she stood peering up at him, her eyes bright and cheery—and in no way affected by the sun. His suspicions confirmed, he frowned. So, she was sharper than she appeared, and a scam artist in her own right. "Looks like I'll need to keep a close watch on *two*…MacBrides," he muttered.

"You'll need to do more than that," she said. "The girl you're eyeing six ways to Sunday is my granddaughter, Kerry Anne. Haven't you noticed the family resemblance?" She cackled a laugh and turned away.

Good thing he wasn't facing a jury right now, because he'd abruptly lost the power of speech. No wonder, back in the game room, Kerry Anne had hung so tightly on to MacBride.

With an uncle like that one, he felt for the woman. But that didn't change things. He needed to keep his promise. He had to protect Mom's savings—and everyone else's—no matter what. Surely Kerry Anne would understand.

He slipped on his sunglasses, then crossed the walkway toward her. Even from a distance, he could see her shoulders stiffen. Not very welcoming, obviously. But with any luck, despite the way she'd acted in the game room, maybe he'd found the one sane member of the MacBride family. And maybe, given the right information, she would be reasonable.

If that didn't work, he'd just have to win her over to his side.

As he moved closer, he took the time to appreciate the things about her he hadn't had the opportunity to notice before. A mass of red curls, trembling slightly in the breeze. A firm jaw—trouble there, for sure. A petite figure clad in a dark blue T-shirt and jeans.

He stopped before her. "We meet again. Under better circumstances this time."

"You think so?"

A tough one. But he'd never met an unwilling witness he couldn't crack. "In neutral territory, then."

No response, as expected.

In the bright sunshine, her scattering of freckles tried to fight their way through the dusting of makeup she'd brushed across her cheeks. He bet she'd look great without the cover-up. Hell, she was cute enough now.

Although, *cute* didn't accurately describe her combination of kiddie freckles and grown-up curves.

"You—" He cleared his throat and tried again. "I hear you're Maeve MacBride's granddaughter."

"That's right." She jerked to such ramrod-straight attention she gained another inch in height. It still didn't bring her to his chin level.

"Then that makes you Brendan MacBride's niece."

"All my life." It looked like she wanted to add something else, but instead clamped her soft lips into a hard line and stared at him.

"Pleased to meet you," he said mildly.

She blinked.

"Have you got a minute? I'd like to talk." He gestured to the bench near the clubhouse.

She looked at him with narrowed eyes for a moment before moving without a word to take a seat on the bench.

He sat beside her, deliberately dropping into a loose-limbed, nonconfrontational sprawl and planning to ease into the important things he needed to say. "I don't know how much you and your uncle have discussed this…project your uncle's come up with. You do realize he's taken money from a group of unsuspecting people." *So much for easing into the topic.*

She shifted away from him and crossed her arms. "They didn't seem unsuspecting to me."

"You weren't there for the beginning of the meeting. Or for the conversations that went on before that."

Her brow crinkled as she frowned. Obviously, she thought things out about as well as her uncle did—which meant, not at all.

"Look, Kerry Anne—"

"Just Kerry."

"And just Matt. Kerry, you're a reasonable woman, I'm sure. Think how you would feel if a relative of yours had tied up her savings in a risky proposition like this one."

He'd figured Maeve MacBride had lent financial support to Bren, possibly using funds she couldn't afford to lose. Kerry's expressive face told him he'd guessed right. A little more straight talk, and she would be his.

"You know, I said it before," he began, "the whole idea was doomed from the start."

"What do you mean?"

"You can't renovate property without following city ordinances."

One corner of her mouth twitched. "I'm sure Uncle Bren's aware of that."

"Then there are the required licenses and permits. And

following up with contractors to make sure the construction is in compliance."

"Of course."

He frowned. "There are all kinds of regulations governing the running of a business."

"Aren't there always?"

The ready responses irritated him. The woman hadn't a clue what she was talking about. "Taxes, payroll, accounts payable."

"Well, naturally."

The smug tone finally did him in. Didn't she realize the enormity of the situation? "And your uncle planned to do all this with money he'd gotten from a scam."

She hissed an indrawn breath and stood. *That* had shaken her, all right.

The news had shaken him, too, when he'd first heard it from his mom. After all he'd done to help her safeguard her finances, to keep her secure, she'd been taken in once again, this time by a silver-tongued scam artist without a conscience.

He had to make the woman in front of him understand. He stayed seated, giving her the power position. Petite as she was, though, they still almost met nose-to-nose. Her blue eyes sparkled dangerously.

He wanted only to stand there and admire them, yet he somehow managed to jump into speech before she could start the rant she so obviously intended. "You expect me to do nothing, when my mother—along with a whole community of people—have had their money finagled out of them by that con artist?"

"Con...? How dare you! You barely know my uncle Bren."

"I know the type," he snapped. "I see them often enough in court."

"Well, maybe you spend too much time there, Counselor.

My *uncle's* heart's in the right place." She glared at him. "Do you even have one?"

A bird chirped, then went silent. The drone of an airplane overhead faded away. In the long silence that followed, he could swear he heard his watch ticking.

"Okay," she added finally. "That was rude. Sorry. But you haven't given him a chance."

"He's had enough opportunity to take advantage of people, especially vulnerable women. They've all sunk money into this venture—"

"Willingly, it sounds to me."

"—probably more than most of them can afford—and the end to the financial drain won't be anywhere in sight. Thanks to that sna—" He caught himself. Why was this woman getting to him? More than likely, because she was related to the snake. "Thanks to Brendan MacBride," he continued softly, "who's spearheading this so-called project. And judging by what I've seen so far, he couldn't succeed at supervising a charity hall bingo game."

"Why not? He's got plenty of enthusiasm about his idea." She stopped, mouth open, then shrugged and went on. "All right, maybe he jumps into things with both feet before thinking them through. And maybe he doesn't have the greatest organizational skills. But you can't condemn a person because of a few faults."

Matt rose and stared at her without answering.

Her freckles disappeared entirely in the flush filling her cheeks. She shook her head, starting those red curls tumbling.

"You've got to give him some time to get things rolling."

"Thirty days."

"What?"

"Thirty days," he repeated, shoving his sunglasses firmly in place. "I'll give you that much time to find a buyer."

The flush drained away, leaving her freckles standing out on her ashen cheeks like blood spatter in a crime scene photo. "W-what do you mean, a buyer?"

"Someone to take that white elephant off his hands—for enough to pay everyone back."

"That's ridiculous. He can't—"

"He'll have to, if he doesn't want to face a lawsuit."

She didn't respond, just stood staring at him so intently, he could almost hear the gears turning inside. She was up to something. Finally, to his surprise, she put her fists onto her hips and glared at him.

"Thirty days won't be nearly enough to get the park in shape. You'll have to give him the summer."

"Now, *that's* ridiculous. Every month that goes by, those people lose interest income."

The gears churned again. "Okay." Her voice wobbled, and she cleared her throat. "Sixty days, then."

He took a deep, steadying breath. He wanted that money back. *All of it.* And she was right—MacBride would never get this settled in a month.

"Agreed. Sixty days to make the sale. Or," he added, trying not to snarl, "I'll do whatever it takes to see your uncle before a judge."

Turning, he stalked away and across the parking lot to his Jeep. He slid into the driver's seat, slammed the door and cranked the motor.

Jaw locked into place, he pulled out of the lot, refusing to look in the rearview mirror. Not wanting to think how he'd backed down, when there was so much at stake here.

Hell, he'd gone into law to protect the innocent. To fight for truth and for justice. He didn't see a whole lot of either one in evidence here. As a result of MacBride's wheeling and dealing, most of the residents of Lakeside Village, including his mom, had zeroed out their savings accounts. That's what he had to focus on now.

He couldn't let Kerry MacBride get to him.

But as he drove away, her image traveled along for the ride. An image of her fists clenched and shoulders stiffened in defiance.

And of her bright blue eyes widened in shock and dismay.

Chapter Three

After a ride back to Chicago she barely recalled and a restless night, Kerry worked out her aggression the next morning by packing away art supplies in her classroom. The students had already finished, but the teachers had this final day to close up shop for the summer.

A summer that was starting off much differently than she'd planned.

She could hardly take in what had happened. Out of nowhere the afternoon before, a perfect stranger, so handsome with his dark good looks and tailor-made suit, had become the enemy. How else could you describe someone who wanted to put your uncle in jail?

Frowning, she shoved an armful of art books into a storage cabinet.

Matt Lawrence was wrong about Uncle Bren; that went without saying. She couldn't help resenting the man for his attitude. And for his part in derailing her schedule.

Still, no matter how reluctantly, she couldn't help but admire him, too. Obviously, he cared about his mother and about all the other residents at Lakeside Village. He was watching out for them, just as she was defending Uncle Bren. But, she thought with a shiver, it was exactly what she admired most about Matt that made him a threat to her family.

She wouldn't let this latest disaster ruin everything. Not

this time. She would go home for the weekend, do what she needed to do, then continue with her life as she'd intended.

"Bet you're loving this day, huh, Ms. MacBride?"

Startled, Kerry looked up at the teenager perched on the ladder in one corner of her classroom. She'd forgotten all about him. "The end of school, you mean?" she asked.

J.J. rolled his eyes. "No—the end of me."

"Oh, I don't know." Despite her worries, she didn't have to force her smile. "I have to admit, you've made some progress since the first day you strolled in here."

Laughing, he jumped down to the floor—a short drop for J. J. Grogan, the tallest, lankiest ex-gang member she'd ever had in one of her high school art classes. And the most talented of all her students.

"Yeah, remember?" He self-consciously adjusted the baseball cap he wore backward, the cream-colored fabric pale against his brown forehead. "Me coming into Intro to Art with my sawed-off Number 2 pencil, thinking we were gonna sit around all semester drawing pictures of naked women."

"And me bursting your bubble with the very first sentence of my opening lecture."

"Yeah." He shook his head. "I almost got up and headed out the door."

"Really? I'm glad you didn't."

Nervous as she'd been that first day on the job, a student walking out would have devastated her. Instead, over the years, she and J.J. had learned and grown together.

"I'm proud of you, J.J. Lots of students have talent, but none of them worked as hard as you did. You *earned* that scholarship."

"Yeah." He shrugged and turned to the job of sorting clean paintbrushes into old coffee cans.

Praise embarrassed him, so she didn't push.

"Bet you're all ready for Europe, right, Ms. MacBride?"

"Right," she admitted, knowing the fellowship was a dream come true. And knowing how well he understood that. Hours studying with master artists. Trips to famous museums in Paris, Florence and Milan....

J.J. lived and breathed art just as she did. It had made him the excellent student he'd become.

And, to her surprise, her love of art had made her a good teacher. Though she'd taken the job originally as a compromise, a way to help support her family while still having time for her dream, she'd found working with her students more rewarding than she had expected.

Teaching kids in this high school was the goal; reaching them became her mission.

"Your granny okay with you leaving for the summer?"

"I haven't had a chance to talk to her yet." Because of a superstitious fear, one she didn't want to admit. A fear that telling anyone in her family would destroy her chance for success. She couldn't let that happen. Frowning down at the table, she added, "I'll be seeing her this weekend."

J.J. grew still. "What's up? You sound weird. She sick or something?"

"No, she's fine." More or less.

Since J.J.'s freshman year, she'd shared bits and pieces about her eccentric family as a way to get him to open up. She hated to reveal the latest news but wanted to be honest with him. "Uncle Bren's here for the summer, staying with Gran again. He wants to renovate an old amusement park in Lakeside."

"Hey, great! That would be some fun place to work."

"You think?" She nodded weakly. "Maybe so. But it's not a done deal yet. There's a lawyer fighting the project."

Unfortunately, J.J. knew all too many people in trouble with the law. "That's bad," he said, staring wide-eyed at her and shifting his ball cap back on his head.

She recalled Matt Lawrence's unsmiling stare as he stood in front of her and shoved his sunglasses back in place. "Yes, it's very bad."

"What're ya gonna do?"

She shook her head and sighed. "What I always do, J.J.," she admitted. "Damage control."

They stood silently for a moment, then she grabbed another armful of books to shelve. "But don't worry about that. Let's talk about you. What are you going to do to enjoy your last summer before college?"

He shrugged and looked back to the paintbrushes.

"What is it?" she asked.

"Nothin'. Just want to help you get this stuff packed up before you get out of here."

Now he was the one sounding strange.

"J.J., what's going on?" She set the books down again and faced him over the broad surface of the art table. "Are you worrying about handling college this fall?"

"Maybe I'm not even going." His tone edged into belligerence.

"J.J., you have to!" The thought of all the advantages he would be risking overwhelmed her. "You've got a free ride for four years—and more important, too much talent to throw it all away. Don't give up your dream when you're so close to reaching it."

He said nothing, just kept stuffing paintbrushes into cans.

Her hands chilled. She pressed her fingers together. Could his unusual reluctance to talk mean something even worse?

Before he had set foot in her classroom his freshman year, she'd been informed about his unstable home life and his gang affiliation. It hadn't been too long ago that he had walked away from that kind of activity. But in this part of Chicago, sometimes walking away wasn't enough.

"J.J." She braced her hands on the table and waited until he met her eyes. "You're not back with Benny and the guys, are you?"

"*No!* I told you, I ain't going that way again."

"Then what's bothering you?"

"Nothing, Ms. MacBride. Stop, all right?" He waved his arm as if trying to push the subject away, knocked against an empty paint can and toppled it onto the floor. The clanging noise that resulted sounded both loud and ominous.

"J.J.!"

Ignoring her, he left the room at a run.

She sagged against the table, knowing she could never catch up. No matter how much he denied it, J.J. was upset about something, something he wasn't handling well alone. He needed help.

The words she had said to him echoed in her mind. *Don't give up your dream when you're so close to reaching it.*

She was so close to hers, too. She couldn't give it up. Not again.

But how could she help J.J. when she'd be leaving town for the summer?

How could she help anyone, when she'd be an ocean away?

A FEW HOURS LATER, Kerry stood in her apartment kitchen, shoving perishables from the refrigerator into a plastic sack to take down to Lakeside with her.

If anything else could go wrong with the beginning of her break, she didn't know what it would be.

J.J.'s angry departure that morning left her worried she'd mishandled the situation. A lot of that was going around.

Facing off toe-to-toe with an irate lawyer the afternoon before—and insulting him, for good measure—wasn't the smartest thing she'd ever done.

Sacrificing her first weekend off to help work up the proposal for the amusement park wasn't any better.

But what other choices could she have made? In both cases,
she'd responded to save her family. Lord only knew, she didn't
want to *be* like her family. But she loved them. All of them.
And they needed her.

She didn't have any options.

And now, with her bag packed and her portfolio ready for
the weekend trip, disaster had struck once again. Her second-
hand sports car, always temperamental, had gotten her *almost*
all the way home from school that morning before deciding
to break down.

Which meant she didn't have any way of getting back to
Lakeside, either.

Though Gran hated the cell phone Kerry asked her to carry,
thank goodness she had answered it when Kerry called.

If anytime had been good for her to back out of her promise
to come home, to unpack her travel bag and repack it with
clothes for her trip to Europe, just then would have been perfect. But Gran had taken away *that* option, too, suggesting a
friend who was visiting in Chicago could give Kerry a ride.

Gran had sounded practically giddy with relief when she
relayed this news. So, she wasn't as comfortable with Uncle
Bren's idea as she'd been letting on. Kerry couldn't back out
now.

Gran had barely blurted out the pickup time—two o'clock—
when the phone line crackled and sputtered, and her voice
disappeared in a noisy haze of static. Then the line went dead.
After that, Kerry hadn't been able to reach her again.

Gran *did* have a point when she complained about the
unreliability of cell phones.

The doorbell rang. Out in her tiny front hall, Kerry plopped
the plastic sack with the last of her perishables onto her
suitcase.

She swung open the door to greet the man who had agreed to take her back to Lakeside. To her dismay, she found herself staring into a familiar pair of mirrored sunglasses.

Her jaw dropped. She couldn't help herself. "You!" she said scathingly.

"You!" Matt Lawrence echoed, not sounding any happier than she did.

"What are you doing here?" she demanded, glaring at him.

"Getting trapped in another of your family's crazy ideas, evidently."

His attitude stung. So did his answer, but how could she deny it? "You mean Gran phoned *you?*"

"Ah." He smiled grimly. "No, my mother called. But now I know who set me up. Not that I had any doubt to begin with. There were only a couple of likely suspects."

Kerry tossed her head and counted to ten. By fives. "Sorry to inconvenience you, Counselor. And for your wasted trip. I'll find my own way back home, thank you." She reached for the door and pushed.

He raised his hand to keep her from shutting him out on the stoop. "What are you going to do, hitch a ride?" He looked pointedly over her shoulder at her suitcase, art supplies and groceries.

A rustling noise came from that direction, followed by a plop and then a splat.

She whirled around. A half-full carton of eggs had slipped from the sack and smacked against the floor, spewing whites and yolks and eggshells across the ceramic tiles.

She whirled back. "How did you *do* that?"

He laughed, loud and long, a deep, full-bellied vibration that shook her with its familiarity. His laugh produced the same effect on her as the music she loved to listen to when she was most immersed in her art. Drums and chants and gravel-voiced lyrics in a throbbing primal beat.

A wave of heat eased through her. She tightened her grip on the edge of the door.

That laugh was dangerous. So was the man.

"You think I've got extrasensory powers?" He smiled.

You've got power, all right. She struggled to focus.

"All I have," he said, leaning closer, "are the wheels to take you home."

And a low, sexy laugh to take me other places.

"You might want to clean things up," he suggested.

She started, stepped back. The ability to move objects *and* the power to read her mind? She could feel that heat, no longer languid, rising into her cheeks.

"The eggs," he added, gesturing toward the hall behind her. "You wouldn't want to go off and leave them."

"Oh…no. No, I wouldn't." Glad for the excuse to get away, she turned and fled from the entryway and down the hall to her small kitchen. Immediately, she grabbed several paper towels from the roll, dampened them with cool water, then put them to her cheeks.

Forget the eggs. She had another mess to clean up first.

She tried not to think of Matt or his sexy laugh. *Or* his fascinating eyes. Hazel, she'd finally realized only minutes ago, as she'd stood toe-to-toe with him when he'd removed his sunglasses. Hazel eyes that changed color depending on his clothing color—and the intensity of his emotions.

Speaking of intensity… She dabbed the paper towel over her face. When she finally felt her temperature returning to normal—or at least as normal as it was going to get around him—she went back down the hall armed with fresh towels and a bottle of cleaning spray.

Matt was gone, and she sighed in relief. Then she noticed

the door stood open and her suitcases and art materials and the rest of her groceries had vanished along with him.

Much as she'd like to believe he'd turned into a simple sneak-thief who had taken off with her belongings, she would never get away that easily. Not with family problems, and not with men.

As she cringed at the thought, a flurry of unwelcome memories bombarded her. Dates that ended badly once either of her older brothers crossed her path. An engagement that had been broken after her fiancé had met her entire family....

Footsteps rang out on the front steps. She dropped quickly to a crouch, bent over the splattered eggs and attempted to concentrate on the messy cleanup.

"Almost done?" Matt asked.

"No, they're still runny."

He let loose a chuckle, briefer than his laugh but packing just as much punch. Keeping her head down, she wiped the floor and fought for a distraction.

Why had she made that remark, anyway?

Because she couldn't help herself. Because she'd hoped for the result she had gotten. Because she wanted to hear that deep, sexy laugh again.

Furious, she scrubbed at a floor tile, as if that would obliterate her thoughts.

"I've got your bags in the Jeep," he said from over her shoulder. "We'd better get on the road before it gets too congested."

She stopped scrubbing and stared at the floor, now cleaner than she'd had time to get it in weeks. Her car wouldn't be ready until Monday—by which time Uncle Bren could be scrubbing floors in some prison, if the man standing a yard away from her had his way.

Reluctantly, she rose to her feet. "I'll be with you in a minute."

"Good."

"But I'll need to make a stop on the way out of town."

He frowned. "How long of a stop?"

"Not very."

"Because the I-57 in late afternoon is no place to be."

Neither was sitting trapped on the highway in a moving vehicle beside this man for three solid hours. Or more, if they didn't get out of town soon. He'd called it right about the congestion.

Even if they did outrun rush hour traffic, she felt sure this afternoon's trip would be the longest ride of her life.

Chapter Four

Know your enemies from their incisors out, one of Matt's law school professors had taught him. *Know your opponents in legal matters even better.*

The woman sitting next to him, her red curls bouncing in the breeze from the open window, didn't look like either one—but was, in actuality, both.

No problem.

Prosecutors and his fellow defense attorneys alike agreed upon only one thing: to get answers to his questions, Matt Lawrence could charm, cajole or coerce words out of a department store mannequin.

No rush now, though. They had just half an hour of their ride behind them and a long time left ahead. And the only thing they had in common was the one subject they couldn't discuss.

It was going to be an interesting trip.

They'd already made the detour she'd requested, to a section of the city he wouldn't normally visit. He'd insisted on going into the rundown apartment building with her. When he had seen the beer-toting guy in the sweat-stained undershirt who answered her knock on the battered door, he'd felt doubly glad he'd gone along.

To her credit, when the guy had promptly responded to her question regarding the whereabouts of "J.J." by scowling, muttering, "The bum ain't here," and slamming the door closed, she turned on her heel and stalked down the stairs and outside to the Jeep without a word.

"Tough luck," he'd said, "not finding your friend home."

Probably annoyed with him for insisting on going with her, she hadn't bothered to respond to his subtle play for info.

He wouldn't push it. For now. His curiosity about her interesting friends would keep. He had enough to worry about with her family. "Too breezy with the top down?" he asked. "I can raise it again and put the AC on."

"No, thanks. Sunshine and fresh air feel good for a change. I work indoors all day long."

"What do you do for a living?"

"Teach."

"At the elementary level?"

"High school."

"Really?" He chuckled. She shifted abruptly in her seat. "The kids must tower over you."

"Not all of them," she snapped.

Sensitive about her height, then. Touchy where her family was concerned. It *was* going to be an interesting afternoon.

"You like the job?"

From the corner of his eye, he saw her shrug.

Body language speaks volumes, that wise professor had told them.

Obviously, Kerry MacBride's actions said she spent far too much time around teenagers.

Matt could read the twitch of an arm or the blink of an eye as well as any lawyer. But he couldn't spend time staring at her—as easy as that job would be—and get them safely to Lakeside during early rush hour. Right now, verbal responses from her would have to do.

Again, no problem.

Kerry couldn't have known it, but the dead-eyed, deadpan

expression he turned on her had left witnesses on the stand quaking in fear, knowing he'd zeroed in for the kill. "You wanted to make a difference?" he said offhandedly. "Change a few lives? Save a few souls?"

"What's wrong with that?" She turned to look at him, her entire body shifting sideways as far as the seat belt would allow. "Why did you become a lawyer? To wear three-piece suits? Find a captive audience? Act out your aggression?"

Bull's-eye. And quick, too.

He gripped the steering wheel and stared straight ahead. Not that any of her wild suppositions had hit the mark, but the leading question had shot home. Why he had become a lawyer was nothing he planned to share with her.

When the witness catches on, change your tactics.

With an effort, he loosened his grasp on the wheel for a second and raised his hands in the air in surrender before putting them back in place. "Let's try this again, why don't we. Teaching's an honorable profession, and I'm sure there are as many reasons for going into it as there are teachers."

Slowly, she leaned back again. A crosscurrent of air swept through the Jeep, tumbling her curls in even wilder confusion around her face and shoulders.

This time, Matt was the one to shift abruptly in his seat.

"You teach art?" he asked, hazarding a guess as he recalled the black portfolio he'd put into the rear seat.

"Yes."

"And you're an artist yourself?"

"Trying to be. It's a tough profession."

"I'd imagine it's about as challenging as being a teacher but more competitive?"

To his surprise, she laughed, low and restrained, as if she hadn't meant to let it slip. "Some days, I'm not so sure."

"What made you decide to go into teaching?" Another

surprise—the question had come out of a genuine desire to know.

"You can't live off your art, not until you make a name for yourself. Meanwhile, you need some income. For me, that's teaching, which fulfills other parts of my creative life."

"Why high school?"

"I like working with advanced-level students, watching their talent develop." Her face softened at the words. She cared.

"Found any Michelangelos yet?"

He'd barely completed the question before she'd bounced into her squared-shoulder position again. If they'd been standing outside instead of sitting in a moving vehicle, she'd have been toe-to-toe with him. But nowhere near eye-to-eye. The thought almost made him smile, but that wouldn't match what he planned to say. Or what he was trying to do. "Hey, I'm serious."

She eased back.

He never typecast people, but she sure had the temper of a redhead.

"One promising student, maybe," she said grudgingly.

"Good?"

"Better than that. J.J.'s got talent, real talent."

J.J. The person they'd stopped to see was actually a kid she taught at school.

After a quick glance at her, he returned his gaze to the road. Did she know how her expression changed when she talked about her students? Or maybe her love of art brought about the reaction. For a moment, he wished…for something he had no business thinking about with this woman. He had no time in his life right now for anything other than work. And looking out for his mom's best interest, of course.

Know your enemies…

"So, J.J.'s promising," he said.

"His craft's still crude," she admitted, "and his knowledge isn't as extensive as it could be."

"The masters have to start out somewhere. They don't all begin by painting ceilings, right?"

She chuckled. "Some of them, like J.J., start by painting ceilings, walls, mailboxes, anything that will stand still."

"Graffiti's illegal."

"Yes, Counselor." He didn't look but knew without a doubt she had rolled her eyes at his obvious statement. "But, done in the right places, it's both legal and a method of artistic expression."

He snorted, then hoped the traffic noise had drowned out the sound.

"And," she added loudly, probably indicating she'd heard, "sometimes, it's a way of communicating with the world."

"Communication? As in, defacing public property—often to the tune of hundreds of thousands of dollars in the manpower and materials needed to clean it up?"

"As in, reaching out in the only way some of these kids know how."

He shook his head.

She exhaled an exasperated breath. "Just because you grew up in comfort—and continue to have all the advantages in life—doesn't mean all kids do."

"I didn't—" He clamped his jaw down on the words. Again, she'd come close to pushing one of his hot buttons.

"Yes, I know." Her voice had suddenly grown flat, drained of all energy. "You didn't mean to imply anything negative. You know those kids are disadvantaged. You know they need help. I've heard it all before. From people who don't believe— or intend to follow through on—a single thing they say."

"You don't know enough about me to know what I believe and what I don't."

"Actions speak louder than words."

"I've heard the cliché. What's your justification for quoting it here?"

She exhaled twice as forcefully as before. "It'll be justifiable homicide here in a minute," she muttered.

Despite his anger, he had to swallow a smile.

"Observe the evidence," she said in a louder, slower tone, the words spaced as if he had trouble with multiple syllables. "Look at what you did yesterday. Threatened a man old enough to be your father—and for no reason."

"What?" Forget the smile. He glared at her, then looked back at the highway. All right, he'd gone over the top the day before. But he'd definitely had his reasons.

"Then," Kerry continued, indignant, "you libeled him to his own niece by calling him a con artist."

"Libel is written. That would be slander—"

"Whatever."

"—*if* the comment weren't true."

"You see? There you go again," she said, sounding smug. Ten to one, she'd used the wrong word on purpose. "And to paraphrase your argument back at you," she added icily, "you don't know enough about Uncle Bren to determine what he is and what he isn't."

She grabbed a floppy-brimmed straw hat and plopped it on her head. The gesture lost a level of its drama when the hat trapped some of her wildly flying hair in front of her face.

He didn't know whether to laugh or pull over and let her out on the side of the road.

A cell phone rang, and after a moment fighting with her hair, she dove into the canvas bag she had thrown onto the floorboard.

"Hello…? Nice to hear from you, Professor…. Yes, I'm looking forward to it *very* much…."

Matt eavesdropped without blinking an eye. In these close

confines, he could hardly avoid doing so. The icy tone she'd used with him had disappeared entirely.

"Oh, that would be wonderful. I'm honored to be included."

She kept her voice level, her words professional, but when he shot a look toward her, he could see the unrestrained excitement filling her face. "Cute" Kerry Anne had suddenly become beautiful. Breathing deeply, he jerked his attention back to the road.

"Yes, I'm sure I could change my flight… *Oh*."

The word plummeted like a parachutist with a defective rip cord.

"I didn't realize it meant coming so much earlier…. Yes, of course. But I can't get away this weekend…. Yes, I know—he makes appearances so rarely…. No, it's a family matter. I can't leave this soon."

He risked another look. The excited expression had faded.

"Yes, I'm very sorry, too…. Yes, I'll be there as planned. Goodbye."

She clicked off the cell phone and sat staring at it, her eyes downcast, her face brooding.

Matt gripped the steering wheel to keep from reaching out to her. "A problem?" he asked.

"No." She dropped the cell phone into her bag. "I'm taking a nap. Wake me up when we get to Lakeside." She sat back against the seat and closed her eyes. "Please," she added, the word sounding anything but polite.

She'd reverted to the icy tone she had used with him before her phone call.

He bit his tongue.

So much for charming, cajoling and coercing the opposition. If any of his partners had eavesdropped on their conversation the way he'd listened in on her phone call, he'd have never lived it down.

He spent a minute wondering why she'd looked so disappointed over that conversation. And why she wanted to see her law-breaking student, J.J. Then curiosity about her situation gave way to irritation. Kerry Anne and her conniving relations had given him problems of his own to worry about.

First, by putting his mother's financial security in serious jeopardy.

Second, after barely an hour, by having come within inches of upsetting his famous equilibrium. Of making him blurt out things he never said.

To anyone.

A space opened in the lane beside theirs. After a glance in the side mirror, he slid into the gap.

With luck, traffic would let up after they'd passed the next major exit, then he could finally get the Jeep moving within range of the legal speed limit.

The sooner he took care of this investment fiasco—and got away from Kerry and her family—the better. But before he drove away from Lakeside again, he'd make damn sure he left secure in the knowledge that he'd done right by his *own* family.

STANDING FROZEN IN THE doorway of Lakeside Village's game room, Kerry felt all too aware of Matt Lawrence breathing down her neck. When she had seen Uncle Bren's car outside the clubhouse and asked to get out of the Jeep there, she'd never dreamed Matt would follow her inside.

Never imagined the chaos they would find.

The room looked as if a twister had swept through it. Twice. Boxes and bags and unidentifiable objects balanced on the edges of the pool tables, leaned up against the walls, and littered almost every inch of floor space.

On the far side of the room, Uncle Bren stood behind one of the pool tables, staring at them.

Taking hold of her shoulders, Matt gently moved her aside. The warmth of his hands seeped through the fabric of her worn T-shirt. Distracted by the momentary pleasure, she didn't realize he planned to cross the room until it was too late.

By the time she kicked into gear, he had his hands braced on the pool table, giving the impression of a hunter who had cornered his prey. From the look of wide-eyed panic on her uncle's face, he agreed.

"What is all this, MacBride?" Matt asked, his voice gentle.

Gentle and *Matt* made a dangerous combination.

Kerry rushed to join them.

Uncle Bren frowned, as if seeing everything around him for the first time. "Supplies. For the park."

"Do you have receipts for all this?" Matt asked. "Did you get the okay from your investors before you spent *their* money?"

Uncle Bren stepped back a half pace. "They're fine with whatever I do."

"No matter how ineptly you do it?"

"Matt, really!" Kerry moved past him and focused on Uncle Bren. "Where are you planning to store all these packages?"

He shrugged.

"You haven't even thought *that* far in advance, have you?" Matt demanded. Shaking his head, he turned to Kerry. "I rest my case. And forget what I said about running a bingo game—this guy couldn't carry off a bake sale if they were giving the goods away."

"Hold on, lad—"

"I'm not your lad," Matt snarled.

Kerry winced but stood her ground. Maybe once they got the shouting over with, they'd have everything out of their systems.

False hope, and she knew it. If she didn't keep them away from each other, Matt would be the one going to jail.

For murder.

No matter how much it hurt her to admit it, Matt was right. Uncle Bren didn't have the skill—or, more honestly put, the stick-to-it-ness—to run a project like this one. The amusement park restoration would turn into a lost cause. So would any chance of his giving the residents their money back.

As the yelling continued, she closed her eyes, trying to conjure up visions of Paris…Florence…Milan….

The images wouldn't come.

She'd lost them, just as she'd lost the fellowship years ago when her family had run into the "wee bit of bother" with their landlord. *That* fiasco had resulted in her canceling all her plans to help them straighten things out.

Not this time. She wouldn't make that sacrifice again. They could have this last week from her, that was it.

She reopened her eyes and focused on Uncle Bren. Wrinkles framed his face. His cheeks sagged. In a mere twenty-four hours, he seemed to have aged twenty years.

"You've not got half a clue—" he was protesting.

"And you haven't got a chance in hell," Matt cut in, "of succeeding with this insane idea."

"You're right," she said, as startled as they were by the words coming from her.

What else could she say? After one brief look at Uncle Bren and one even quicker look into her heart, she knew she was doomed.

She couldn't change her family.

She couldn't change herself.

Even if it meant having to give up her summer. Having to

turn down the fellowship she coveted. And, once again, having to walk away from a chance to fulfill her lifelong dream.

"You're right," she said again, looking from one man to the other, finally letting her gaze rest on Matt. "Uncle Bren won't be overseeing this project. *I* will."

Chapter Five

Maeve MacBride nodded approvingly at the stopwatch she'd used to time her early-morning jog across Lakeside Village's tree-shaded common area to Olivia Lawrence's apartment.

"Not bad for a youngster of eighty-three," Maeve said to the younger woman. "At this rate, I'll win the next Senior Sprint running backward."

Olivia didn't reply.

The lack of response worried Maeve. She didn't like being beholden to anyone. But she needed Olivia. The only consolation was, Olivia needed her even more.

Maeve scanned their surroundings. The clubhouse sat squarely in the middle of the common area, which was bordered on the east and west by individual homes and on the north by a squat, redbrick apartment building. The south edge of the common sloped down to the lake, now mirror-bright and blinding from the reflected rays of the rising sun.

Rainbow's End had disappeared in a shimmering haze.

She looked back to the apartment. Olivia owned a one-bedroom unit on the top floor, plenty of space—in Maeve's opinion—for a woman who lived alone.

Only she wasn't exactly living alone this morning.

Matthew Lawrence's Jeep sat in the visitors' parking lot in the space closest to Olivia's front door.

"Where's that lad of yours?" Maeve asked, trying not to sound suspicious.

"In the shower." The other woman glanced quickly toward the building and back again.

Maeve frowned. "Now, don't tell me you're coming down with a case of cold feet." With the amount of effort she'd put into this plan, she didn't need Matthew's doting ma to mess things up.

Olivia shook her head. "No, it's not that. I just never thought Matthew would take all this as hard as he has. I should have known, though. He's always so vocal about anything he sees as an injustice."

"He was loud enough about it the other day, for sure." She frowned again. Olivia hadn't said anything about his stubbornness when she was singing the boy's praises.

Albie Gardner's interference at the clubhouse had thrown a spanner into things, too, but nothing she couldn't handle. As long as she kept Olivia on track.

"You know what you're supposed to do?" she demanded.

Olivia nodded. "I just hope I can pull this off. Matthew's not easy to deceive."

Maeve patted her shoulder. "Get your thinking straight, lass. We're not deceiving him, we're just letting him keep his innocence a while longer." She laughed. "You've got the easy part, after all. If you think your Matthew's hard to take in, you ought to try my Kerry Anne. It was a close call hanging up that awful cell phone on her yesterday, then having to ignore the ring when she called back. And, not to mention, playing cat and mouse with her since last night."

"I don't really like going behind her back—"

"Olivia!" Maeve thrust out her hands imploringly, nearly losing her grip on the stopwatch. "We'll not get anywhere if you keep fiddle-faddling around like this. Kerry Anne's been up before dawn, getting all her ducks in a nice, neat row. But we need to keep her innocent, too. There's a lot at stake here, love—for those two *and* for you and that lad of mine. Don't you know that as well as I?"

"Of course I know it, Maeve." She frowned. "But I'm also not too happy about playing this 'poor little woman' role."

"Then the sooner we do what's needing to be done, the better."

"Yes, ma'am," Olivia said, raising her right hand to her temple in a brisk salute.

Maeve chuckled. "It's off with you now."

She made shooing motions and stood watching until Olivia walked across the common area and entered her building.

The lass had spunk, you had to hand her that. If anyone could put the starch into Brendan's shorts, she would.

Kerry Anne presented more of a challenge—but it was just the kind of challenge Maeve liked.

Still, as she eased into a quick heel-to-toe power walk, she shook her head in mild frustration.

How in the world did these younger generations ever manage on their own?

KERRY KEPT A TIGHT hold on her clipboard.

After spending most of last night and half of this morning coming up with a proposal to present to the residents, a game plan for getting the park into shape, she acknowledged that she might just be the slightest bit cranky from lack of sleep.

Looking away from Uncle Bren and sending her gaze around the game room gave her the few seconds she needed to calm herself. More or less.

She'd been shocked when neither Matt Lawrence nor his mother had shown up for the meeting this morning. Matt's absence especially made her uneasy. Only because she didn't know what he was up to, nothing else. At least the meeting had gone well. Her proposal had been accepted, and she was on her way to getting an inventory list in hand.

"Okay, where are we supposed to put all this stuff once I've logged it?" she asked, trying not to think how right Matt had been when he accused Uncle Bren of not thinking far enough ahead.

Why she'd jumped to defend her uncle, she really had to wonder. He meant well—he always did—but the reassurance did nothing to make her feel better. Her late-night inspection of his limited paperwork proved he had gone forward with the plan to renovate the amusement park the same way he went ahead with all his ideas—operating on a wish and a whistle in the dark.

"No worries, Kerry." He beamed at her now. "We can store this in one of the buildings out on the pier."

"Uh-uh." She shook her head. "Not until we make sure they're secure. We wouldn't want vandals taking off with everything."

"There aren't any vandals in Lakeside," he began, then saw her expression and stopped. "All right, then. Ma ought to be able to find room."

"With me taking over her couch and Brody in his sleeping bag on the floor because you're borrowing his bed? Not a chance."

Colin and Brody, her two youngest brothers, still lived at Lakeside Village with Gran. At twelve, Brody loved the new sleeping arrangements, but with Uncle Bren and Kerry both home now and taking up space, Gran's house didn't have an inch of room to spare. Kerry sighed so deeply, the papers on her clipboard ruffled in the breeze. "I'll talk to the manager about some temporary storage area. At least, things are looking a little better in here."

She turned her attention back to the room.

After the meeting, when a dozen or so of the neighbors

had volunteered to lend a hand, she had jumped on their offer. Then she'd literally rolled up the sleeves of her cutoff sweatshirt and begun organizing the material. *Someone* had to make order out of the confusion.

"Uh, Kerry…what about Olivia's boy?"

"That lawyer?" She forced a laugh. "Don't worry, Uncle Bren. I'll handle him."

Poor choice of words, there. She turned, hoping he hadn't noticed her reaction. At the thought of *literally* getting her hands on Matt Lawrence, the entire clipboard had trembled.

How she could feel even the tiniest bit of interest in him amazed her. How she could feel the depth of attraction she *actually* did—toward the man who wanted to ruin her family—made her ashamed.

Taking a deep breath, she got a grip on the paperwork again. And on herself.

"All right, what about the receipt for these packages here, Uncle Bren? You know we're going to have to account to Matt for every penny you've spent."

No answer.

She turned back to where he had stood just moments before, only to find the space empty and the patio door of the game room swinging closed.

"As usual," she muttered, low enough so the residents on the other side of the room wouldn't hear. "When the time comes to get down to work, Uncle Bren disappears." She shoved her pencil through her hair. "And now where did Gran go off to?"

"You'll be tripping over me in half a moment, Kerry Anne, if you're not careful." The much-loved voice, soft and lilting, came from behind her.

Kerry suddenly found herself enveloped in the trademark

lavender scent that could bring her back to her childhood in an instant. Unfortunately.

She turned to eye her grandmother, so delicate with her fluffy white hair and ruffled dress and soft woolen wrap. So dainty and slight at only five foot one, an inch shorter than Kerry.

And so devious once you got to know her.

"Oh, hello, Gran." She raised an eyebrow. "Just the person I've been wanting to see—and alone, for a change. Funny, wasn't it, how I couldn't get you by yourself for a minute this morning?"

"Not a bit, Kerry Anne." She glanced down and shifted the straps of the canvas knitting bag she carried almost everywhere. "You've been busy since you arrived here last evening."

"And you've been avoiding me since then."

"Not at all. Whatever has you thinking such nonsense?"

"Oh…I don't know. Maybe because I saw you practically spoon-feeding the boys their cereal this morning—and they're twelve and fifteen?" She wouldn't be at all surprised to discover Gran had roped the two boys in on the evasion. "And after that you disappeared and I couldn't find you anywhere."

"I went out for my morning jog."

"*Went* out? Or *skipped* out? Because something tells me you wanted to avoid having the chat I mentioned last night."

"Oh." Gran raised a hand to her cheek. "I'd simply forgotten all about it, love."

Kerry smiled wryly and gave her a quick one-armed hug. "Save it for a stranger, Gran, because I can see right through you. *Nothing* in this family is simple, and you know it. Now. What was the idea of sending Matt Lawrence to my house yesterday?"

"You needed a ride, and he was in your area."

"And how did you know that?"

"Olivia."

"His mother?"

Gran nodded. "He's a fine figure, isn't he? And Olivia says he's a bachelor, never been marr—"

"*Gran.* You can't possibly be trying to *fix me up* with him? Are you—" She bit off the words. "You know he's ready to throw Uncle Bren to the wolves the first chance he gets."

"Oh, fiddle." She hoisted her bag to her shoulder. "Nothing but a bit of bluff."

"I wish *I* could be as certain of that."

"Trust me, Kerry Anne. The lad wouldn't hurt a hair on anyone's head."

"Says who?"

"Olivia. And if you're not believing his own ma…" She paused, as if waiting for Kerry's assurances.

"I can hardly believe someone I've never met."

Gran's beaming face glowed like the man in the moon's. Instantly, Kerry felt a twinge of unease.

"As I say, if you're not believing Olivia's words—" Gran gestured toward the other side of the room "—then there's someone else you can ask."

Kerry turned her head in the direction of the door leading from the patio. The same door Uncle Bren had escaped through, minutes before.

Only instead of her uncle returning to help with his own project, there stood Matt Lawrence, all six-foot-plus of him, dressed in jeans, T-shirt and boots.

Ignoring the little throb of pleasure pulsing through her, she muttered, "Darn, what's he doing here? I'll never get anything done if I have to play referee between that lawyer and Uncle Bren."

Gran didn't respond, and a quick glance proved she'd slipped away as quietly as her son had. Reluctantly, Kerry dragged her gaze back to the man across the room. Matt looked good. *Very* good.

Of course, she'd had enough experience with her own family not to trust appearances.

Matt Lawrence might have left behind the fancy business suit and polished shoes for this trip to Lakeside, but his casual clothes didn't change anything. He was too much of a lawyer. Too intense about his beliefs. Too ready to start trouble.

And, she noticed to her dismay, he had just set his sights on her.

MATT STEPPED OUT OF the path of a couple of determined-looking women carrying small packages across the game room.

They weren't the only ones hard at work, and things looked considerably more organized than the mess he'd seen littering the place the night before. Clearly, the petite redhead with the no-nonsense manner on the opposite side of the room had handled the transformation. She got things done. And she cared about people. Her family, the residents here, her students. Too bad, in this case, she'd lent her support to a lost cause.

He looked around the area again and found no sign of MacBride. The man's niece would have to do.

Not a bad trade-off, at that. Even from this distance he could see the bright blueness of her eyes. And the calculation in her gaze. He found anticipation rising as he headed toward Kerry MacBride.

The woman's misguided family loyalty annoyed the heck out of him. Still, her feistiness offered a challenge. The way she stood now, with her feet planted and a clipboard held in front of her cutoff sweatshirt, showed she had geared up for battle.

No problem. Courtroom, game room—the venue didn't

matter. He never backed down. He just utilized different methods of dealing with different enemies.

He gave her a genuine smile. "I see you've rallied the troops around here, gotten a little action going."

Curls bounced with her curt nod. "Yes, we're doing fine. Thank you for noticing."

"Always the keen observer, that's me."

"And the eager volunteer?"

He shook his head. "Sorry. Not for this joke of a project."

She ignored the comment. "So then you've shown up only to bother me?"

"Is that an admission?" He leaned closer and murmured, "*Do* I bother you, Kerry Anne?"

He was rewarded by a flush of color staining her cheeks.

"Kerry to you," she snapped.

That flush had come from anger, then. Not from the slow rise of pleasure—

"Kerry," he snapped back, equally as angry—with himself.

What was he doing, wasting time with thoughts like that about this woman when he had business to take care of? Though he could hardly get down to the bottom line when MacBride hadn't shown up yet.

"My mom and I were out all morning," he continued. "When we got back, she sent me on another errand. And when *I* got back, she was gone. Something told me this might be a likely place to find her. But no luck." He narrowed his eyes. "I've also noticed there's no sign of your uncle around here."

"My." She blinked rapidly several times. "You *are* a keen observer, aren't you?"

He couldn't help but grin. "I try. So, what's the story? He's lost interest in his own scheme already?"

The clipboard jerked to attention. "It's not a scheme. And, in case you've forgotten, I'm in charge of the renovations now. Which reminds me, I've got to see the manager. If you'll excuse me…"

Before he could react, she sidestepped him.

"Wait up, I'll go with you."

Her gaze shot to his. "Why?"

"I'd like to speak to the man myself. It's a free country, you know."

"Yes," she agreed, smiling, "where people are innocent until proved guilty." She started away from him, adding over her shoulder, "You might want to stay here. I may be a while."

"That's okay. I'll just soak up the atmosphere while I'm waiting." He followed in her footsteps, admiring the view of paint-spattered jeans and a thin line of pale skin showing beneath the edge of the sweatshirt. From the back, he could see she'd caught her hair in a gold clip and crisscrossed two pencils through the mop of auburn curls.

Unaware of his scrutiny, she led the way into the hallway and down to the office at the opposite end of the building. Outside the office door, a large carton rested on the floor, limiting passage through the hall. They walked around it and entered the room. Inside, a woman stood thumbing through a file cabinet drawer. At the sound of their feet on the tiled floor, she turned to them.

"Morning, Alice," Kerry said. "Is Don around? I'd like to talk with him."

"No. But…"

The woman looked past them to the doorway. Matt sidled up a half step closer behind Kerry, indicating they were together. Alice barely glanced at him.

"Kerry, he isn't a bit happy about Bren putting all those boxes and things in the game room. He didn't want to take it up with Maeve, but he's planning to come in later today, even though it's Saturday, to track down your uncle."

In front of him, Kerry's shoulders stiffened. The clipboard snapped up toward the sweatshirt again.

"Fine, Alice. Exactly what I wanted to talk to him about. I'll see him then."

The bright tone she'd tried for came out sounding brittle, to his ears at least. Alice must not have noticed, because the frown lines between her eyes disappeared. "And, Kerry—" she gestured over their shoulders "—he wants that box in the hall out of here. As in yesterday."

"No problem." The brittle tone again. "I'll take care of it right now."

Again before he could react, Kerry made a move, whirling toward the doorway, then stumbling backward when she found him standing so close to her.

He reached out quickly to grab her forearms, then wished he hadn't when his palms registered the sensation of warm, supple skin. Her eyes met his for a split second before she pulled herself away.

She dropped her clipboard onto a nearby chair and went out into the hall.

This time, following in Kerry's wake, he felt suddenly like a water skier losing control behind a runaway boat—and he didn't like the sensation one damned bit.

Chapter Six

Matt actively disliked everything about the entire situation he'd been forced to step into. Except, maybe, this woman.

This woman, who had been coerced into things she'd rather not be involved in, either. This woman, who had somehow gotten to him in a way he couldn't explain or understand. All he knew was, she raised emotions in him he didn't want to feel. He had to get his mind back on business—right now.

"Kerry." He reached for her, this time taking care to make contact with sweatshirt fleece before resting his hand on her shoulder. "Hold on a minute." He kept his voice down, mindful of Alice in the next room. "This whole situation is ridiculous. We have to talk."

Once they set foot back in the game room, there'd be no chance to see her alone. Although, judging by the skeptical expression she turned his way now, his chances of talking her into a resolution to the problems her uncle had caused might have been better if he'd cornered her where there were witnesses.

"I have work to do. Honestly, I don't have time to stand around arguing."

"But you'll take on an irate manager later today, just to save your uncle's hide?"

"Why not?" One corner of her mouth quirked up. "I'm getting plenty of practice with an irate lawyer."

Yeah, he had to admit she had a point. What made him effective in the courtroom might have him sound unintentionally ruthless in private conversation. Time to change his tactics. "Yes," he said very calmly. "My argument exactly. I don't understand why *you* should have to do anything, when it was someone else who created this entire mess."

"Then there's no use my explaining, is there? Because if you haven't caught on by now, you'll never get it."

"Look, I'm only trying to give you an out."

She nodded. "Thanks, but I can take care of myself."

The sound of a file drawer sliding closed followed by Alice's footsteps crossing the tile floor cut off anything he'd have said next.

Kerry stooped down to pick up the short but wide carton near the door. Her look of chagrin as she tugged on the package told him she couldn't handle it alone.

Alice appeared in the doorway and eyed him.

His gaze ping-ponged from one woman to the other. He never reneged on his word, and he'd already said he wouldn't lift a hand to help. Looking down at Kerry, he shook his head, realizing he didn't need to back down on his original statement. Judging by her struggle, he'd have to offer *both* hands.

"I'll take an end," he told her.

"Not necessary," she said from between clenched teeth.

"Of course it is. My mother raised me to be a gentleman."

Alice giggled.

Smiling grimly, Kerry said, "Fine. Let's get to it, then."

As she reached for a better grip on her edge of the carton, the ragged neckline of her sweatshirt dipped downward, showing off a few golden-brown freckles but stopping short of anything tempting.

Just as well, because he wasn't interested.

Crouching, he reached for the other end of the package.

They lifted it from the floor, grunting in unison as they rose.

"What did your uncle put in here?" he demanded.

"Bodies, I think." Her grimace revealed one slightly crooked tooth off to one side. *Cute.*

The carton was too wide for them to walk side by side. Slowly, he backed down the hall, heading toward the game room. "You know we could get arrested for hauling cadavers around?"

"Where are you from," she asked, "the permit police?"

"No, but I've got friends in the department."

"Why do I find that hard to believe?"

"That there's a permit department?"

"No," she said, puffing with exertion. "That you've got friends." This time, the crooked tooth flashed in a fake grin.

"Very funny. Just my luck to get stuck with a comedian."

Breathing more heavily now, she simply rolled her eyes.

"Do you want to stop and take a break?" When she shook her head, he adjusted his grip to take as much of the weight as possible from her. "What makes you think we'll get this to fit through the doorway?"

"If it doesn't," she said between gasps, "I'll make it fit."

He had a feeling she would, too. He laughed and eyed her over the top of the box. Again, he saw the slight flush that almost erased her freckles. He wondered if it came from anger this time.

They'd reached the game room, and he maneuvered himself backward into the doorway.

"We've got to hike it up to clear the plate on the frame," he told her.

As they did so, his partner lost her grip on the box. It slid sideways and jammed in the doorway.

"It's all cockeyed," she said. He didn't need to see her face; he could hear the breathless indignation. "It's got to be straightened out first."

"No kidding. I'm trying." The weight of the carton made it awkward to juggle from one end.

"Kerry Anne, is that you out there?" called a woman from the room behind him. He recognized Maeve MacBride's voice.

"Mind you don't put your back out, love," she continued.

No concern for his back at all.

He might've expected that. After all, Maeve was Brendan MacBride's mother.

He returned his attention to the woman out in the hall. The woman he might never see again, if he didn't get this carton out of the doorway.

Just as he gave an extra-hard tug, he heard an extra-loud grunt from his partner. The box shot toward him, sending him backward and almost off his feet.

"Easy, lad," said Maeve.

Something sharp prodded his shoulder. Was she resorting to stabbing to get him out of the picture?

Ignoring her, he helped Kerry right the carton and guided the rest of it through the doorway.

"Over by the far wall."

He didn't much care for her barked order, but after a quick look at her flushed face and the damp curls corkscrewed on her forehead, he decided not to argue. Instead, he eased the carton to the floor.

Groaning, she stood up, stretching all five feet and a couple of inches of her, rested her hands on her hips, and arched her back. The move created a bigger dip in the neckline of her raggedy sweatshirt. How far down did those freckles travel, anyway?

Maeve MacBride came up to them, toting a canvas bag.

From the top of the bag protruded a pair of knitting needles—her weapon of choice, more than likely. He contemplated bringing her up on charges. Anything to provide a distraction from his latest thought about Kerry.

Maeve stood shaking her head. "You'll be needing a soak in the tub tonight, Kerry Anne."

So much for distraction. Instantly, he envisioned Kerry in nothing but a damp towel and a cloud of corkscrew curls.

"As for *you*..." Maeve said abruptly, turning to him.

He jumped. Hoping like heck she hadn't read his thoughts, he cautiously looked her way.

"Not bad," she said, taking a small, colorful object from her bag and slipping it into his T-shirt pocket, then giving his chest a tap. "We haven't seen a good day's work out of you yet, but I imagine that'll happen soon enough."

He ignored whatever she'd put in his pocket. Chances are when he pulled it out, it would self-destruct in his face. He was beginning to get the idea that *all* the MacBrides were dangerous, each in their own special way.

"I don't think you ought to get your hopes up, ma'am. Carrying one box doesn't mean I'm going along with the plan."

She laughed softly—and he'd heard friendlier sounds coming from convicted felons. "You might find yourself wrong there, laddie. There's being convinced, kicking and screaming. And then there's being brought around gently to another way of thinking."

His old law school professor had told him that once, and the concept had served him well since then. Maeve MacBride climbed a few notches in his estimation—until she glanced from him to Kerry and smiled.

He glanced from her to Kerry and frowned. His stomach thumped, twice, as if he'd swallowed that pair of weights he never had time to use.

Pink-cheeked again, Kerry turned away.

Chuckling, the older woman followed.

He stood there, shaking his head.

Maeve wasn't thinking of hooking him up with her grand-daughter, was she? He wasn't about to get involved with a woman until he'd made partner and could consider himself secure.

Although, he had to admit that Kerry was pretty cute.

Well, all right, Kerry MacBride was beautiful. He'd ac-knowledged that to himself yesterday during their ride back to Lakeside and reinforced the observation only minutes ago. She had a sexy grin that turned him on and a sharp wit that got him going, too.

She also had an unscrupulous uncle he'd sworn he would take down. That's what had gotten him here in the first place and what had brought him back again. *That's* what he needed to focus on.

Not beautiful Kerry MacBride and her sexy smile, but the pending disaster that would bring everyone to ruin.

A disaster brought on by the complete incompetence of the man who had just appeared in the game room doorway.

"OH, NO," KERRY GROANED under her breath.

She refused to turn back to look at Matt, who now followed at her heels. She hadn't yet recovered from dealing with him out in the hallway before Gran had brought her down with her sneak attack. Her cheeks were still burning from Gran's remark to him.

The lawyer already had a bad enough opinion of her family.

Besides, she didn't want him second-guessing her. She didn't want him feeling pity for her. And, most of all, she didn't want him thinking she could only get dates if they were arranged by her grandmother!

Now, looking to the other side of the game room, she

braced herself. Without a doubt, this situation was about to go from bizarre to unbelievable.

Uncle Bren and Matt's mother crossed the room toward them. Finally, Kerry had the opportunity to observe the woman up close. She looked about Bren's age, putting her near sixty, with salt-and-pepper hair in a trendy short cut and pale, perfect skin.

The growl coming from Matt confirmed Kerry's suspicions that things were about to turn ugly.

"Matthew." His mother hurried toward him. "Sorry, I'm a little behind schedule. Brendan and I needed to discuss a few things. I thought you'd planned to meet me at the house."

"I tried that. When I got back from picking up your prescription, you weren't there."

"Oh." A becoming pink blush suffused her cheeks.

"Meanwhile, I had some business I wanted to take care of here."

"I see." She shot a worried glance from one man to the other and finally settled her gaze halfway between them. "Hello. You must be Kerry. I'm Olivia Lawrence. I've heard so much about you from Brendan."

"Hi."

Matt's growl revved up to the sound of a cement mixer.

"And from Maeve, too, of course," Olivia rushed on, as if afraid her son would break in. Or more afraid of what he would say if he did.

The man didn't seem to have much patience with anything.

Sure enough, he stepped forward a pace.

"MacBride. About time you showed up." He looked at the crowd around them. "We need to talk. Alone."

She'd wondered where Uncle Bren had gotten to earlier, after he'd somehow slipped away when she wasn't looking. Or had she been hoodwinked by Gran? As horrible as it felt to think that of her own grandmother, she knew it might not be far from the truth.

In any case, she wished Uncle Bren had stayed away. He'd taken a belligerent stance with hands fisted and chin raised. A problem just waiting to happen. Yet, even as she winced at the sight, his gaze skittered away from Matt, as if he'd suddenly become afraid of facing up to this lawyer who meant nothing to them but trouble. The reaction bothered her, and all her protective instincts jumped to the fore.

Somehow, she managed to clamp down on them.

Matt had been nice to her; he'd helped her. For a brief time, she'd even dared to hope they might manage to work together. But he had said it himself. Assisting her with one box didn't mean he'd joined their cause. She had to remember that. And she had to support Uncle Bren.

"Wait a minute." She put her hands on her hips and turned to Matt, looking up to make sure he met her eyes. "First of all, can you lower your voice, please, before anyone else notices?" So far, her volunteers had stayed busy at their tasks, and the last thing she wanted was to draw attention if he planned to start renewing his threats. Considering the state of their finances, she desperately needed those volunteers.

That thought pushed her forward.

"Second of all," she said to Matt, "any discussion you need to have with Uncle Bren, you can hold in front of me. Especially if it concerns the amusement park."

"I can't guarantee it will be fit for a lady's ears."

She exhaled abruptly, forcing the most unladylike snort she could manage. "You know where I work. There's nothing much you can say I haven't heard a student say before."

"Maybe your students don't consider you a lady." He glanced toward his mother.

And maybe Matt didn't, either. No big surprise there. No one ever did. With Sean and Patrick born before her and Colin and Brody coming after, she'd focused more on keeping up with the boys than on developing any feminine wiles. She'd been a tomboy forever, probably always would be. Still, the idea that this man might have classified her after a few hours' acquaintance set her temper alight. She could get her Irish up as well as Gran could. But that wouldn't help the situation. Fighting for control, she pressed down so hard with her hands, she practically fused them to her hips.

"What is it you've got on your mind?" she asked evenly.

Olivia took Uncle Bren's arm and moved him closer, putting the four of them almost shoulder-to-shoulder in a small circle.

Kerry felt like the runt of the litter.

"Matthew—" Olivia began.

"Mom, let me take care of this," he said, his gaze locked on Uncle Bren. "MacBride, it's bad enough you've thrown innocent people's hard-earned money away on a run-down pier, a scattering of ramshackle booths and a handful of amusement rides all battered and rusted beyond repair. And now you're too busy—" his gaze shot to Olivia, then back "—even to lend a hand with this decrepit amusement park?"

Kerry looked at him in surprise. Matt's argument hadn't presented anything new, but this last angle certainly had. Could it be Uncle Bren's friendship with his mother that had him so upset now?

His voice had risen, and his deep, rumbling baritone projected easily into the room. It must come in handy in court. Just as Kerry had feared, the residents started to gather around.

"It's not decrepit." Indignation filled Uncle Bren's tone. "Why, if you'd only come take a stroll around the park like we asked—"

"To see what? That the buildings look about to collapse, and the pier's likely to give way any minute?"

Kerry flushed. For just an instant, she felt light-headed enough to give way herself. Even from a distance yesterday, she had noticed how run-down the old park looked. Matt had a point, she had to admit. The investors could be in over their heads. But she couldn't let him browbeat her family. "How do you know what the park looks like, if you haven't seen it up close?" she demanded.

"I don't need to—"

"Excuse me." A slight, deeply tanned man had stepped closer to their group. "The pier is steady as they make them."

Matt frowned. "And you know this, how?"

"A good eye—"

Matt laughed.

"—and forty-eight years in structural engineering."

Kerry turned to him in relief. "Thank you, Mr...."

"Call me Carl."

"What about the buildings?" Obviously, Matt wasn't going to let this go. "You can't tell me they're not in bad shape."

Another man stepped forward, as tall and broad as Carl was slight. "Weather damage, that's all. Some wear and tear, but nothing a handful of two-by-fours and a coat of paint won't fix."

"And you know—" Matt began.

"Fifty-three years in construction," the man interrupted, a smug smile creasing his broad face. "And *you* can call me Mr. Delmont, sonny—*if* you have to call me anything at all."

Kerry choked back a laugh. The smooth-talking lawyer had been outtalked—and outfoxed—by a couple of small-town seniors. Evidently, the knowledge didn't sit too well with him. A slow burn of color crept across his cheekbones.

Her hand suddenly itched for a pencil and her sketchpad.

Uncle Bren gave her a tentative grin, which brought her back from her artistic fantasies immediately. If he'd known all these positive things about the park, why hadn't he said something *before* Matt threatened him with jail?

"All right," Matt said in a tone so unexpectedly soft, a few of the residents moved closer to hear. "If the property's not totally derelict, that ought to make it easier to sell."

His mother touched his arm. "Oh, Matthew—"

"Sell?" Uncle Bren roared, drowning her out. "What are you thinking, lad? We threw that idea out long ago."

Matt froze. So did Kerry.

The room settled into a breathless silence.

Several long seconds later, he turned slowly in her direction, his eyes wide in disbelief.

A wave of guilt washed through her. She hadn't yet been able to bring herself to tell Uncle Bren—or anyone else— about Matt's sixty-day ultimatum. She didn't want them digging in their heels over it. But she'd convinced the residents it was in their best interest to fix up the amusement park and sell it for a profit.

At least, she *thought* she had.

Still, she raised her chin defiantly. "I presented the proposal this morning. It passed."

"Totally *uuuuu*nanimously," Uncle Bren put in. "We're keeping the park."

Trust him to make the situation worse!

"But, Uncle Bren," she began, "we didn't say anything about keep—"

"It was after you went to the office to get that package," he mumbled, then turned back to Matt. "We've just told you the place is fit for running. We've all agreed on it, too."

"Fine," Matt snapped at him. "My original argument stands. So, get the place up and running—that will make it easier to find a buyer so you can refund my mother's money."

Olivia Lawrence opened her mouth, but before she could say anything, Matt turned on his heel and walked away. His long-legged stride carried him across the room and out of Kerry's sight before she could do much more than blink.

Olivia met Gran's frown with a resigned shrug. Obviously, the woman knew her son.

The gesture confirmed Kerry's worst fear.

Matt wouldn't budge on his ultimatum. Especially not if Uncle Bren and Olivia had unknowingly pushed his concerns to another level.

Part of her—a tiny part—couldn't help feeling sympathy for Matt. She would fight just as hard, if she thought someone wanted to take advantage of her family. And clearly, he had suspicions along that line.

But one look at the shock on Uncle Bren's face and the fire in Gran's eyes told her she had to do more than stand there flapping her eyelids.

Chapter Seven

After taking a deep breath and stalking to the doorway, Kerry stared down the hall, where Matt paced furiously enough to wear the flowers off the carpet.

Chicken that she was, she waited until he was striding away from her before following him. Unfortunately, before she could think of what to say, he made an abrupt U-turn and nearly ran her down. She almost tripped backing up a step.

"Your grandmother shoved this in my pocket." He raised one fist between them, then spread his fingers wide to reveal a wad of multicolored wool resting on his palm. "What the heck is it?"

"It's a green bag."

"It's *not* green." His expression clearly showed he found her as nutty as the rest of her family.

"I mean, it's green as in recycled. Gran's very big on saving the environment. It's a shopping bag—she knits them by the dozens and gives them out to everyone she meets."

"What a letdown," he said, his tone loaded with sarcasm. "Here, I thought I was special."

You are *special.* She wished she could say those words.

"Umm…Matt. Can we talk a minute? About those empty threats you keep making…?" When she saw the hardness in his eyes, she faltered but pushed herself to go on. "You wouldn't have my uncle put in jail. You couldn't."

"Couldn't I?" His lips curved upward.

Her heart gave an erratic double beat. From stress, no doubt. Her blood pressure was probably sky-high from this fiasco, too.

She wished she could fade away, like the trampled flowers worn beneath Matt's feet. But she had to save Uncle Bren. And strange as it seemed, in order to do that, she'd have to fight this lawyer over a cause she didn't fully believe in.

She braced herself and began her argument. "You use expert witnesses in the courtroom, don't you? You heard those men in there. They might be retired, but they're retired *experts*. If they say the pier and the park are in good shape, why won't you listen?"

"Because this has been a crazy idea from the start. Most amusement parks don't break even, let alone make a profit—especially small local parks like this one. This entire deal is taking advantage of unsuspecting people. And their money. And I feel compelled to add, I'm not impressed by the under-handed way things are done around here." He leaned toward her, his face set in grim lines. "Like getting that proposal passed."

She shrugged. "The meeting was for the property owners, and you're not one of them."

"My mom is, unfortunately."

"Yes, but we had a majority vote, with ninety-nine percent of the owners here. Your mother was the only one missing."

"That was convenient."

"Wait a minute." She froze. "Do you think I deliberately held the meeting when she wasn't around?"

"No. More like, when *I* wasn't around."

"You heard Uncle Bren—even I wasn't there when they decided to go ahead with running the amusement park." Anger mixed with another wave of guilt. She hadn't set up the meeting with Matt's absence in mind, either, but she *had* been happy to present her ideas without him there. She didn't need a rabid lawyer breathing down her neck. Or becoming a distraction.

As if things hadn't already gone beyond that.

"I'll work on them," she conceded. "I've got sixty days—"

"Fifty-eight."

"All right, fifty-eight. Until then, you've got to lighten up a little, Matt. The world—and this project—doesn't revolve around you. And if you ask me, your mother looks perfectly capable of taking care of herself. You make it sound as if she's too fragile to dress herself in the morning."

Again, color slowly suffused his cheeks. His hazel eyes darkened. "I'm a better judge of what my mother can and can't handle, don't you think?"

Hold your tongue.

The warning came too late. The situation had stressed her too much.

Emotions welled up inside her. Disappointment and resentment over the upset to her summer plans. Anger at the way Matt treated her family. And irritation at Uncle Bren, too.

A regular storm of sensations she couldn't—maybe didn't want to—control any longer.

She was tired of always being the peacemaker. The fixer. The one who saved her family from themselves.

She was so tired of always having to bite her tongue, swallow her words, tamp down her temper, and make everything right for everyone—everyone but herself.

For once, she just wanted to let her Irish rip. And Matt had given her a perfect opening.

"Since you've asked," she began, keeping her voice pitched low with an effort, "what I think is, you spend too much time judging people. You're not content with being a legal eagle. You want to be judge, jury and chief jailer." Proud of her control, she softened her voice another notch, proving she could be calm and reasonable—even if *he* found the idea too much of a stretch. "Your attitude's not right, Matt. And it's not necessary."

He laughed without humor. "Yeah? Try taking a look at your uncle and saying that with a straight face. If not for you, this entire project would sink like a stone into the lake."

Above the angry buzzing filling her ears, she heard footsteps behind her. Her next words caught in her throat. Praying that neither Uncle Bren nor Gran had heard Matt's statements, she whirled around and found herself facing Matt's mother.

Judging by Olivia Lawrence's wide eyes and pale face, Matt's taunt had affected her as much as it had Kerry. The older woman sent her a glance of agonized apology.

"Let's go, Matthew," she told him. "We'll be late for my appointment." Taking his arm, she half pulled him toward the exit doors.

He looked over his shoulder at Kerry. She straightened her spine and stood with her chin up and her lips pressed together. But her eyes narrowed against the spike of pain shooting through her temple.

Matt's mouth opened as if he wanted to say something else.

Before he could speak, Kerry turned and walked away, not wanting to hear another thing from him. Not willing to give him the satisfaction of seeing her left alone, defeated, in the hallway.

Defeated? *Ha.*

Maybe she should have stayed behind and let that lawyer think he had bested her. Assuming he'd won might cause him to loosen up, to let his guard slip a bit.

At the thought, yet another pang of guilt shot through her.

That devious idea had sounded exactly like one her crazy family would have come up with.

But if Matt thought he could threaten, scare or dictate to her, he had a few more thoughts coming. He didn't know Kerry Anne MacBride at all.

Or how far she would go to save her crazy family.

SEETHING, MATT STRODE along the sidewalk.

The conversation with his mother wasn't going at all the way he'd planned. Irritation ate at him, lack of control made him more abrupt than he intended. Worst of all, worry about her had him stumbling over his words—a hell of a thing for a normally glib lawyer to have to admit.

He gestured with both hands in frustration, found he was still carrying crazy Maeve MacBride's green bag, and shoved the stupid thing into his back pocket. "Mom, why can't you see it? It's obvious this project's nothing but a scam, and you and all your friends have thrown good money away on it. It's just as clear this MacBride character's a loser."

"Don't you think you're being harsh on him?"

"No," he said bluntly, and meant it.

"Well, *I* do. You know, Brendan is one of those friends you mentioned. And I think he's done a great thing for all of us."

He swallowed his cynical response but couldn't help exhaling in derision.

"Matthew." She rested her hand on his arm, forcing him to come to a stop beside her. She also forced a smile for him, crinkling the skin around her hazel eyes. "I'm sixty, sweetheart, not seventeen. And while I appreciate your concern, I believe I'm capable of judging this situation for myself."

He nearly severed his tongue trying to hold back his instinctive response. That was just the problem—his mom wasn't any kind of judge at all when it came to men. It was up to him to protect her and get her out of this predicament.

"I also believe," she added, "that I did a better job of raising you than appearances seem to show. I heard what you said to Kerry MacBride—"

"All true."

"It might be. But so were some of the things she said to you. You're so *focused,* Matthew. So intent on looking for the bad, you forget there's often good to be found there, too." She gave his arm a quick squeeze. "Now, I really have to get to my appointment. Please, let's go."

She headed toward his Jeep in the parking lot, leaving him with his mouth hanging open.

He snapped it shut and followed her, shaking his head.

What was going on here? He should have been able to handle this disaster the way he handled his cases in court: by outlining a simple, straightforward legal argument that would lead to a clear-cut resolution.

And instead it had come to this.

The MacBrides were making him as crazy as they were. The first woman to intrigue him in years treated him like her worst enemy. And even his own mother didn't understand he was doing what he had to do.

LATE THAT AFTERNOON, the supplies in the game room finally in order, Kerry turned to the next item on her agenda. Clipboard in hand, she headed outside. From there, an easy half-hour stroll around the lake would take her to the amusement park on the opposite side.

In the crowded game room, she had seen the results of Uncle Bren's spending spree, of what he'd bought with the balance of the money contributed from most of Lakeside Village's residents.

Now, she had to find out what he had done with the bulk of the investment—to see exactly what kind of pig in a poke he had gotten everyone involved in. She needed to figure out whether or not they could fix up the property enough to sell it.

But more than that, she had to see for herself the mess Uncle Bren had got them into. It was just her way, ingrained after years of taking care of her family.

She was going to take care of them, as always, and she was going to sacrifice her dreams yet again. The argument with Matt Lawrence earlier had proved to her she had no other choice.

No matter what she told herself about solving this problem and walking way, she wouldn't be able to do it. She couldn't leave her family behind to deal with this themselves. Especially not with Matt around, constantly making things worse.

"In a hurry, aren't you?"

The sound of his voice almost directly in her ear made her jump. She hadn't heard his footsteps on the gravel. He must have cut across the grass from the parking lot to creep up behind her. After their last conversation, she found it surprising he would come near her at all.

"You know," she said mildly, "every time I turn around, you're at my heels." In another situation, from another man, she might have enjoyed such undivided attention. But this was ridiculous. "And I'm only going out to the pier to look around. So I'll be—"

"I'll go, too. It'll give me the opportunity to see just what your uncle's done with the money he's…taken."

"Invested," she retorted.

"Right."

Looking past Matt to the lake, she wished fervently that she could drift away on the breeze-stirred ripples scoring the water's surface. She brushed past him, hurrying down the slope. A big mistake. The uncut grass, thick and slippery, didn't offer much traction. Her feet began to go out from under her. She fought to stay upright, to save herself from a fall.

He reached out to grab her, his hand firm, his fingers

strong, his palm solidly against her skin. Warmth from the contact made her skin flush, all the way up her arm to her neck and into her cheeks, and she knew there was no way Matt could miss it. Just as she couldn't miss the opportunity to look at him this close up, to see the contrasting dark flecks in his hazel eyes and the tiny scar just visible under one of his brows.

For a moment, they stood without moving and stared at each other.

Matt's lips parted.

Kerry took a deep breath and pulled away.

"Looks like it's a good thing I'm out here," he said. "I came to lend a hand—and you might be needing one. Literally."

"Oh, really?" She forced a laugh and started walking down the slope again. Carefully. "I'm not usually such a klutz. But your offer's on the table now, so no taking it back. I just might put you to work at the park."

At the bottom of the slope, they turned onto the well-worn dirt track leading to the lake. Wildflowers lined the path on both sides, straggling onto the walkway and creating a riot of color, catching on Kerry's jeans as she brushed past them and sending up clouds of perfume. Normally, she would have stopped, smelled and touched the blooms, and mentally begun sketching them on paper.

Today wasn't a normal day.

They tramped along silently, sometimes in full light, other times in the shadows cast by the branches of spreading trees. Kerry's skin prickled from the alternating bands of sun and shade. Or so she told herself, refusing to believe she could still feel a reaction to Matt's hand on her arm.

As they closed in on the amusement park, Matt finally spoke.

"You're really willing to risk sending people out onto that pier?" he asked, sounding genuinely concerned.

She eyed the park, trying to observe it through his eyes. Or, at least, from an objective artist's standpoint. Even from this distance, she could see the unkempt look of the buildings, with their exteriors shedding layers of peeling paint and their tattered awnings trembling in the light breeze. But those were incidentals.

"Matt, the pier is safe. You heard Carl this morning."

"You're going to take his word for it?"

"That and his forty-eight years of experience."

They approached the park entrance, a wooden archway with the words *Rainbow's End* outlined in faded lettering overhead.

He looked up, shaking his head.

"What?" She frowned.

"This place is supposed to be someone's idea of a pot of gold? That's what you find at the end of the rainbow, isn't it?"

"I never have," she admitted. "But, yes, so the story goes."

"Well, that's appropriate. It matches the rest of the fairy tales being told around here."

"It's more of an Irish legend, I believe," she said coolly. She came to a stop and turned to him. "Matt, it's obvious you don't want to step foot on that pier. So what are you really doing here right now, anyway?"

"I told you, lending a hand."

She raised her brows.

He laughed. "All right, then, let's say I like to be where the action is. And you seem to be the center of most of it."

"No, the action's out there on that pier. That *safe* pier."

To prove her point, she passed beneath the arch and strode across the weathered planks toward the small wooden ticket booth inside the entryway.

When she heard him following closely at her heels, she

stopped and turned back. "Oh, my goodness," she said, deliberately fluttering her eyelashes. "Aren't you afraid your weight will plunge us into the lake?"

"Very funny." He grinned. "It might, but at least when it happens, I'll be close enough to rescue you."

"I can do that for myself, thanks. But it won't be necessary. And I'm not going any farther than this today." She pulled her clipboard from under her arm and scanned the top—blank—page. Anything to avoid seeing the way Matt's grin lit up his entire face.

She braced the board against the ticket booth's front counter and pulled a pencil from her hair. "It's too late in the day to start anything out here. I'm only going to make a few rough sketches."

"Didn't MacBride get hold of the engineering plans for the property?" Matt asked in surprise.

"Not that I'm aware of," she said shortly, knowing Uncle Bren should have investigated that angle. But when she'd questioned him about it earlier that morning, he'd been clueless. "Besides," she said, hoping to distract Matt from another rant about her uncle's shortcomings, "I want the drawings for me. The visuals will be more helpful in pointing out what has to be done now."

"I can see that for myself already," he said, his face twisted into a scowl.

And how did she know what he looked like, when she was supposed to be focusing on the task in front of her?

"What is it your uncle does for a living?" he asked suddenly.

"Why?" she asked, tightening her grip on her pencil.

"You work in visuals. I rely on words. I'm just trying to get a handle on the man. Maybe the more I know about him, the more I'll understand how his mind works."

"I don't know about that. He's…he's a bit of a different breed."

"Now, *that's* an understatement."

"And I'm afraid that's all you're going to get from me about Uncle Bren. Why are you shining this light on him, anyway?"

He smiled. "Would you rather I shine it on you?"

That stopped her.

"You're probably twice as interesting as he is." He leaned forward, lowering his voice. "Want to share your deep dark secrets with me?"

"Right now, Counselor," she said unsteadily, "I don't even want to be sharing this conversation with you. Why don't you go for a short walk?"

He chuckled. "I think you mean, 'Take a long walk off a short pier.' And the outcome, on *this* pier, wouldn't be a surprise. I'd probably stumble over a broken board and fall into the lake before I got to the Ferris wheel."

"Not necessarily," she said, turning her back to him. "Why don't you give it a try?" To her immense relief, she heard him walk away.

Staring at Matt Lawrence wouldn't get her work done. Unfortunately, he was worth a second look. But she needed to stop indulging her fantasies. No matter how attracted she was to him—and he was a *definite* attraction—they wouldn't stand a chance together.

She and her family were a package deal. Take one, take them all. And despite her loyalty for the MacBride clan, they did come up a few branches short on their family tree. Which made her absolutely the wrong woman for a straitlaced, by-the-book lawyer like Matt Lawrence.

Sighing, she tried to focus on her clipboard and found it too small for a decent outline of anything. Next time, she'd bring her sketchpad.

She looked down the length of the pier in the gathering dusk. There was something about this place that she wanted to get down on paper, then onto canvas. Something in this scene that spoke to her, though she wasn't quite sure yet what it was.

Maybe the feeling came from the simplicity of the wooden buildings with their colorful strips of peeling paint.

Or maybe, she thought with a shiver of unease, the park gave a distorted impression of innocence half-hidden under many layers of deceit.

Not unlike this fiasco of a situation she and Matt found themselves in.

"What's that supposed to be?" Matt asked from behind her.

She shrieked and whirled around, sagging back against the ticket counter. "Why do you keep sneaking up on me?"

"I didn't. How could I, with my boots on these wooden planks?" He demonstrated by rapping his heel on the pier. "You could have asked me to pose, you know."

"What?" She stared at him.

"For the picture."

He tugged on the clipboard, still clasped against her. She looked down at the top sheet in dismay. Most people doodled when they had paper in front of them and nothing else to do. She always used that time to create the first stages of a new piece of art, letting her mind and her hand wander across her sketchpad, tapping into both conscious and subconscious for guidance, inspiration and truth. She would have to control that impulse around Matt.

While her thoughts had wandered to him now, her hands had taken over. On the paper she had sketched his face, including the faint shadow of that tiny scar beneath his brow.

She swallowed hard. "Oh, that," she said, forcing a grin.

"I saw the dartboard in the game room and thought whoever used it next might like a new target."

"Very funny, Kerry Anne." He tried to glare, but the sudden slight curve of his mouth gave him away. "That would have to work both ways, you know."

He leaned closer, smiling, and she pressed back against the counter behind her, hoping it would keep her shaking knees from collapsing. "Wh-what do you mean, work both ways?"

"If you make me a target, I get to set my sights on you."

"Oh." Her laugh sounded as breathless as she felt. "I thought you already had."

"Very observant. And now we've come to an understanding…" He moved in even closer.

Her chin went up in a reflexive response. To argue with him, of course. To set her jaw and announce just what she thought about him—

Oh, no. In view of what she'd been thinking about him only moments ago, that would be dangerous. Her sketch proved that.

But she didn't have time to worry about what to say.

As her chin went up, his came down. His mouth met hers, his lips warm and firm and supple. At first, he brushed his mouth lightly against hers, as if waiting to see if she would draw away. Instead, she lifted herself slightly on her toes, still comfortably braced by the counter behind her.

He gently tugged her toward him, unknowingly taking her away from that steadying surface and, just for a second, leaving her wobbling in midair—a sensation oddly matched by the sudden fluttery beat of her heart. Then his arms went around her, holding her close.

Shivering with pleasure, she realized she'd wanted to be with him like this almost since the first moment she'd seen him, so dark-eyed, tall and handsome. Could it have been only two days ago? It seemed like so much longer.

She told herself—yet again—she needed to keep away from him. He was all wrong for her. He was out to get Uncle Bren. Instead of giving in to attraction, she had to see him as the enemy.

But when he tilted his head, deepening the kiss, she stopped thinking about all that. She stopped thinking about everything.

Except this man and this moment.

Chapter Eight

The kiss was over almost before it began. With a look of horror, Kerry turned away and busied herself with a fresh sheet of paper on her clipboard, plainly avoiding his eye.

The only way to keep *his* eye on this project, Matt had decided, was to keep in close contact with Kerry.

Her uncle might have instigated this entire problem, but without a doubt, Kerry was the one who would bring things to a close. Whether that would happen fast enough to suit him or not, he didn't know, but while he had the time, he intended to stick around and move things along.

He hadn't planned on taking things as far as he had.

What had made him crazy enough to kiss her? He blamed that picture she'd drawn of him on her clipboard.

Obviously, the woman had been thinking about him...as much as he'd been thinking about her. He liked teasing Kerry, sharing the mild flirtation. He'd enjoyed their kiss—maybe more than he should have. But it was a one-time deal. He had no desire to hook up with her....

Okay. That wasn't entirely true. Desire played a part in his thoughts about her, a big part. He wanted a wife and family someday. But right now, there was no place for a woman in his life. Not in that regard.

And when it came to the amusement park plan, no way was he going to let himself get trapped by this softhearted woman. Softhearted with everyone but him, that is. She was motivated by emotions, and that never went down well with him. He was definitely a straight-out facts and figures man.

Though there were other types of figures….

He leaned back against one of the shacks and eyed hers.

The sun was beginning to lower toward the horizon, but nothing could hide her curves or dull the shine of her hair and its several shades of red.

Footsteps echoed on the boardwalk behind them. Matt turned and saw a portly, sandy-haired man approaching. He wore a dress shirt, slacks and a tie settled high enough at the neck to give him a second chin. Lakeside Village's manager, no doubt.

The minute he opened his mouth, he confirmed Matt's surmise.

"Ms. MacBride, I'm told your uncle's somewhere on the premises, but I can't seem to find him anywhere at the Village."

"No sense looking for him here, either," Matt said.

After shooting him a warning look, Kerry turned to the other man. "It's okay, Don, I'm actually the person you should be talking to now."

"Ah. Well. We can't have residents taking it upon themselves to appropriate space in the recreation center—or anywhere else on the property, for that matter."

"Yes, I realize that. I'm working on it. Uncle Bren hadn't known what else to do with the supplies he'd ordered and—"

"What?" The manager frowned at her in clear suspicion. "I thought you just said *you* were responsible for the items left in the game room."

"Excuse me—" Matt began.

Kerry eased toward him, her elbow colliding softly with his ribs. "No, I'm in charge of the renovations over here at the park. The supplies were left there before I came on board and—"

"Well, something has to be done about them. They can't stay where they are."

"Yes, I understand, but—"

"No buts."

"Excuse me," Matt said again, putting his hand lightly on Kerry's arm. Two could play the body-block game.

The man looked over at him and wrinkled his brow, as if trying to decide whether or not he knew Matt. He didn't, and Matt preferred it that way.

"I believe," he began, "that Ms. MacBride is attempting both to explain the situation and to resolve the matter. But we won't know for sure if she's not allowed to finish a sentence."

For a long moment, Don looked down his nose at Matt. Quite a feat, as the man stood no taller than Kerry. Finally, he turned to her. "And what arrangements are you making to move that—that mess from the game room?"

She grimaced. "Actually, I was hoping we could leave it there—temporarily—until we see whether we have a safe storage place somewhere here on the pier."

"Out of the question." He snapped the words so briskly his second chin wobbled. "The room has to be accessible to the residents."

"Excuse me," Matt said for the third time. And the last time. He was done with pulling punches. The man was nothing but a controlling, power-mad…manager who had no right to be so rude to Kerry. "First of all, when were you last in the game room?"

Don blinked. "Late yesterday afternoon."

"Then I think you'll find things are considerably less of a mess now than they were then."

"That doesn't—"

"And," he added smoothly, "you'll also find that those supplies are jointly owned by most of the residents of your community. I can't imagine how they'll feel about having all their property taken from the safety of the Village's clubhouse and relocated out here to the pier before we've had a chance to make sure the area is secure."

"That isn't my problem," Don barked.

"It could be." Matt crossed his arms and stared down at him. He was on shaky ground here. Hell, legally, he didn't have any ground to stand on. But he wasn't about to let this guy keep pushing Kerry around.

"What are you saying?" Don demanded. "They would sue? But *this* property has nothing to do with Lakeside Village's owners."

"Don," Kerry broke in, "I'm sure that's *not* what Matt meant at all. Matt—" she half turned her back to the manager so she could stare up at *him,* her eyebrows nearly knitted together in a scowl, her eyes zeroing in on him like twin gun barrels "—you don't need to say another word. I'll take care of this."

He nodded, holding back a smile. There was just something about her, even when she got riled up. Maybe especially when she got riled up.

He watched as she set her expression into softer lines again before turning back to the other man. Now, why couldn't she look at *him* that way, with that lack of animosity, and mean it? Why was she being nicer to this creep in the choker collar than she'd ever been to *him?*

Over Kerry's head, Matt stared at Don, raised his brows and did what he could to give an impression of innocence. If his acting skills weren't strong, and if Don instead read the expression as confirmation of his own fear about a lawsuit— hey, there wasn't a whole lot Matt could do about it. Kerry had requested that he bow out of the conversation, hadn't she?

The other man frowned. "All right. I'll give you until Monday evening. Then that pile of…supplies goes elsewhere."

"That's fine," Kerry said. "Thanks, Don."

He nodded shortly, eyed Matt without saying a word, then turned and left them alone. Not nearly soon enough.

Kerry gave a huge sigh that ruffled the hair around her face. "I could have handled him, you know."

He fingered one of her curls. "I'm sure you could have. But I didn't like hearing how he spoke to you."

She stared at him for a long minute, her blue eyes softer now, but her mouth turned down in a frown.

"What?" he asked.

"Matt…" She sighed again. "It wasn't any worse than the way you talk to me, at times." Before he could react, before he could pick his jaw up again, she began to turn away.

"Hey," he finally managed to say, "wait a minute."

She looked up at him, and he would swear tears had sprung to her eyes. The sight hit him like a punch to his stomach. Then she tilted her head slightly, and he realized he'd been mistaken.

But the idea he had upset her lingered.

And the fact he couldn't shake the thought upset him.

"I've come on strong a few times," he admitted. "But you have to agree I had valid reasons."

She gave a half shrug, half nod he found somehow endearing.

"You also have to admit," he persisted, "you've given back as good as you've gotten."

"What was I supposed to do? Let you walk all over me?"

"That sure never happened."

She was feisty when it came to sticking up for herself, ferocious when she needed to protect her relatives. How could he blame her for that?

"I'm the only girl in the family," she said, as if by way of apology.

"That explains it, then. Survival of the fittest?"

Her lips quirked up at the corners. "I prefer to think, survival of the smartest. But don't tell my brothers that. And," she added, "I either had to give back or give up—and there *was* no chance of survival if I'd chosen that alternative. So I learned to outsmart them."

"When you were about nine?"

She shook her head. "Six."

They both laughed.

Crossing her arms, Kerry headed toward the park entrance. He fell into step beside her.

"Well," she said, "it's going to be dark out here before long. The supplies will have to wait." Her lips twisted wryly.

Grimace, grin, smile—it didn't seem to matter what she did with that mouth. He liked it.

He stumbled over his own feet as that thought hit him, then almost fell off the pier as another followed.

He wanted to lean down and kiss her again.

KERRY TOOK A DEEP BREATH and tried to ignore the man beside her. Carefully, she walked up the slope outside the clubhouse, not wanting to risk another slip on the thick grass and having Matt reach out to help her again.

The *last* time he'd touched her, he'd kissed her. And her response had told her just how much she needed to stay away from him.

At the top of the slope, the sound of a familiar, tinny ringing brought her to a halt.

Gran pulled her trike to a stop in front of them, barely missing Matt's toes.

Under her lashes, Kerry watched as he took in the sight of Gran in her jogging suit astride her tricycle. She sat in the front seat with a tandem seat for a second rider behind. The trike also sported a passenger car. On the side of the car, a metal sign demanded If You Can't be Irish, at Least be Green.

Matt looked dazed.

"We're meeting up for dinner at Bill's," Gran announced. Bill's Griddle and Grill was their family's favorite restaurant. "You and Olivia, too," she told Matt.

He nodded but said nothing. He just began to wander in the direction of the parking lot.

Kerry would blame his reaction on the sight of Gran's trike, except for the fact that he'd been unusually quiet on their way back from the pier.

"What did you do to him, love?"

"What did *I…?*" Kerry stopped short, recognizing the gleam in her grandmother's eye. "This was your idea, wasn't it? Inviting the Lawrences to eat with us?"

"It was my turn," Gran said, shrugging.

Maybe she simply meant her turn to play hostess. But why did the words sound so ominous? "What do you mean?"

Gran's face twisted in exasperation. "Well, who do you think got Matt out of the way this morning so you could present the proposal in peace?"

"Who…?" Kerry gasped as the suspicion hit her. "Not *Olivia?*" Good heavens, it wasn't bad enough that Uncle Bren had made Kerry guilty by association. Now, her family had corrupted Matt's mother, too.

Gran grinned wickedly and turned away. "Yoo-hoo, Matt!"

He turned back to them.

"You won't mind taking Kerry Anne along with you, will you?"

"Gran," she muttered. Was there no end to the MacBride clan and their schemes?

"I thought I'd pick up my mother—"

"Olivia's all taken care of, and the car's full."

Matt looked pointedly at the trike.

Gran looked back at him. "Laddie, you can't be expecting an old lady like me to haul another body on this vehicle."

Right. As if Gran didn't give Colin and Brody rides to school on that trike on a regular basis. At least, until the boys protested that they'd much rather walk.

She could have argued the point, but she wanted to be with Matt. Alone with Matt—before he had to face the dubious pleasure of dinner with her brothers.

"Well, I'll see you both there," Gran added brightly. "Supper should be a real fun time."

Kerry swallowed her groan.

BITING HER LIP, KERRY hovered next to Matt at the edge of the concrete walkway leading to the restaurant, waiting for their families to arrive.

The squat, square unpretentious building they stood outside didn't look like much, but Bill's Griddle and Grill constituted one of Lakeside's landmarks—and the place to see and be seen on a Saturday night.

The smell of burgers and onions wafted toward them on the light breeze, and she realized how hungry she was. But how would she ever survive dinner, let alone enjoy it, with Uncle Bren and this man at the same table? With Colin and Brody there, too? She couldn't confirm that *any* of her family—including Uncle Bren and Gran—would be on their best behavior.

Come to think of it, she couldn't speak for Matt, either.

And Gran expected to have a fun time!

"Interesting," Matt said, as he noticed Uncle Bren and crew

exiting the car in the parking lot. "Your uncle brought in reinforcements."

"Don't be ridiculous," she told him. "They're my brothers."

"Exactly how many of your generation *are* there in the MacBride family?"

"Five."

"I see two there, and you make three. Then we can expect the rest of the cavalry to show up at any time?"

She shook her head. "Not unless they had a sudden urge to saddle up and ride in to town."

"They've moved away?"

"My oldest brother, Sean, moved to New York after graduation. The next oldest, Patrick, lives here in town. He's traveling on business right now."

"And you've still got the youngest two with you."

"Gran does," she corrected him.

His brows rose a fraction. "I thought this was a fifty-plus community."

"It is. The residents voted years ago to give my grandparents special permission for us because Gran—and Grandpa, of course, before he passed—lived here a long time."

"'Us?'" Again, his brows went up.

This time, she ignored the question and the movement. "I would have taken the boys with me when I moved to Chicago, but I didn't want to upset their lives…any more than already necessary. And I *couldn't* have uprooted Gran if I tried."

"Chicago's quite a hike from here."

"Yes, I know," she said quietly, grateful he hadn't pushed about the issue of her parents. Their lives—and their deaths—weren't subjects she discussed with anyone. "I don't like being so far away. But there were no jobs here when I got my degree, and the money's much better there. I'm able to help Gran out more. I gave her a cell phone so she can always reach me. I'm in near-constant contact and come home a lot on weekends and school breaks."

Why was she spilling all this information? To distract Matt from the fact that Uncle Bren and Olivia seemed much too cozy as they walked along the path from the parking lot? To delay going in to what would have to be an awkward meal with all of them together?

Or because the kiss she and Matt had shared had unsettled her as much as it seemed to have unsettled him?

Even though he'd grown quieter afterward, that kiss had offered her the faintest flicker of hope. Maybe *that's* why she was rattling away like one of her more hyperactive students.

"Sounds like a lot of responsibility for you," he said.

She shrugged. "I do what I have to." *And give up what I have to.* She pushed the thought away. "In an emergency, Patrick's just a few minutes down the road, when he's not on a business trip."

"Then the rest of the time, your grandmother's in charge of those two boys over there?" He waved toward her brothers, now leading the group across the parking lot. "Seems like a lot for a delicate older woman to handle." Gran had just pulled up. "What's with the trike, anyhow?"

"She refuses to ride in anything with a motor. Air pollution, you know. She rode a bike for years, until we all ganged up on her and told her she needed something more stable. Uncle Bren came up with the idea for the trike and made it for her."

"Your uncle—" he began, his brows knitting together.

"You think she's delicate?" she blurted, trying to divert his attention. "Gran's about as fragile as a Sherman tank. You've seen her on the trike. You should watch her taking the boys on at the track."

His eyes widened. "You're kidding."

"Not a bit. She's won more local and state marathons than anyone else in town. Appearances can be deceiving."

He swung his gaze to Colin and Brody again. "Not with those boys, I don't think. They're younger than you, obviously. And just as clearly related." Reaching out, he touched one of her curls. "Who's who?"

"Uh…" For a minute, her mind went blank. *Come on, Kerry. Get a grip.* She shook her head, unintentionally swinging her hair out of his reach. "Colin's the taller one. He's fifteen. Brody's twelve."

Her brothers had moved ahead of the rest and acted as if they were separate from the group. She understood the feeling.

As Matt continued watching them, she concentrated on him.

That twinkle in his eyes wasn't meant for her—no matter how much she might wish that. And, of course, the sparkle wasn't even coming from a genuine emotion inside him, but from the lowering sun. That didn't matter. The sight entranced her, anyhow, in the way the light transformed his irises from hazel to golden brown. It would take a while to mix the right colors, but she could match that exact shade.

And the way the sunbeams played off his dark hair. Now, that would be an interesting use of—

"Find any gray hairs yet?" he asked.

"What?" Her cheeks burned. "I mean, no." She gestured widely, pointing to an oak tree spreading its branches across one corner of the parking lot. "I was watching that humming-bird at the feeder."

"Uh-huh."

Matt had lost interest. Worse, his eyes had suddenly lost their sparkle. He stood glaring, his face turned toward the restaurant. The boys and Gran had disappeared through the open door. Uncle Bren had his hand at Olivia's waist as he escorted her ahead of him.

Beside her, Matt's shoulders strained against the fabric of his shirt. He muttered something she couldn't catch and took a half step forward.

She grabbed his arm. Muscles tensed beneath the shirt-sleeve, tingling the tips of her fingers, making her want to hold on tighter. She stopped herself, barely. But she couldn't stop herself from envisioning him cradling her in the circle of his arms. Cheeks burning, she snatched her hand away. "You're not planning on making a scene in there, are you?"

He turned back. "You're not planning on holding me captive, are you?"

"Reading my mind again?" A second later, she realized what she had said. And how he could take it. Evidently, how he *had* taken it, judging by the way his mouth curled at one side.

She had a vision of that mouth brushing lightly against hers, and a warm, pulsing sensation suddenly coursed through her. She swallowed hard and forced herself back to the here and now.

Even as Matt's mouth smiled, his eyes stayed emotionless, canceling out any indication of humor.

She didn't know which part of his expression to believe—or which was worse. Having him laugh at her words, making her feel foolish. Or having him fake a response, making her angry with herself for caring how he felt.

She knew how *she* felt, too.

Ignoring the heat flooding her cheeks, she raised her chin and stared him down. Up, actually, as he stood a foot taller than she did. "I'll do what I have to do. We might as well get that in the open right now, if it isn't clear already."

"Calm down, Kerry Anne." He held her gaze. "You're a real fighter when it comes to your family."

"Of course. Aren't you?"

She forced herself to look away and head across the walkway, trying not to think about him trailing behind her. Trying not to wonder why, when the sun still sent out strong rays of light from the horizon, his eyes had suddenly looked as if they'd been shadowed by a cloud.

Chapter Nine

Matt followed the rest of his group through the restaurant.

The one huge room was crowded, noisy and smoky from the busy grills. Long wooden picnic tables and matching benches sat in rows up and down the space, with occasional breaks between for aisles that didn't seem wide enough to handle the flow. The decorations ran from weatherworn highway signs to expired and battered license plates, with a handful of old movie posters thrown in.

The boys moved ahead of the crowd, worming their way through the press of bodies, and found a littered table off to one side of the room.

"We're supposed to bus our own tables?" Matt asked in surprise.

"The waitress will be along in a minute," Kerry informed him. "You see how busy they are."

"Yeah," he admitted. The food smelled good, and he felt hungry despite the haze of grease in the air. "A real cholesterol-counter's heaven here," he murmured.

Kerry shrugged. "It's not as bad as it looks."

"It's probably worse." His eyes surveyed the area but his mind was still on her. What could have happened for Kerry and her brothers to lose both their parents already, and so young? He couldn't imagine a childhood without his mom.

His father was another story.

"Hey, people. Let me take care of that." A short, plump woman with a cloth in one hand and a spray bottle in the other made quick work of cleaning the table.

Kerry and Bren followed the two older women onto benches. To Matt's annoyance, that left him with the choice of sitting beside Kerry or her uncle. No contest. He took the space next to Kerry. Brody and Colin promptly filled in the ends of the benches, hemming him in by MacBrides no matter which way he turned.

The waitress left them with a stack of plastic-coated menus. Brody sent them sliding, one by one, along the length of the table. Matt grabbed the last menu before it could slip past.

"Thanks for the service," he said.

"No problem," Brody answered, missing Matt's sarcastic tone completely. He picked up a set of salt and pepper shakers. "I'm gonna be a juggler in the circus when I grow up. Wanna see?"

"Not right now," Matt said quickly.

Colin turned away in teenage contempt at his younger brother.

Brody shrugged and went through the same routine with the salt and pepper shakers that he had with the menus. The saltshaker caught in a crack between two boards of the table and toppled over, spewing white crystals into Matt's lap.

When Brody reached for a ketchup bottle, Matt got to it first and gave him a jaw-locked grin. "Why don't I pass this along?" he suggested.

"That's no fun," Brody said.

"But a heck of a lot safer for those of us on the receiving end." Matt turned to hand the bottle down the table and found Kerry eyeing him. "What's the matter?" he asked. "Did I just break a family tradition?"

"Yes." One corner of her mouth quirked up as if she fought not to give him the satisfaction of a smile.

He found satisfaction in the sight, anyway, even as he wished he didn't. Teasing Kerry, flirting with her, was dangerous. "You guys must be a barrel of laughs at reunions."

"You'll never know how much."

And never want to. But he kept that thought to himself.

At the other end of the table, MacBride had obviously made himself indispensable to his mother, holding out a menu and consulting with her over it as if it held the answer to world peace.

The man defied belief. He exchanged greetings with anyone within shouting distance, knew all the waitresses by name, and generally acted as if he were mayor of Lakeside, or at least owner of this burger palace.

The waitress returned with their drinks and unloaded her tray onto the table between the two boys. Brody reached for the closest mug. Matt looked at him. He looked back.

The kid had red hair, like his sister's, and a map of freckles across his face. His blue eyes, also uncannily like Kerry's, remained turned in his direction for another minute, then finally, the boy lifted the mug and took a long gulp.

Matt drank deeply from his own mug.

"Hiding a smirk?" Kerry murmured.

He put the drink down. "Just thirsty."

"Uh-huh. I saw the staring contest. You do like to get your way, don't you?"

Frowning, he turned to her. "What's that supposed to mean?"

"Just an observation."

"And you're good at that?"

"Observing? I hope so. Artists depend on a trained eye and awareness of their surroundings."

"Teachers probably rely on those even more."

She ducked her head.

"Hiding a smile?" he asked. "You know, you're not the only observant one around here."

"Really?" She tilted her head, arched one brow, met his eyes…then deliberately looked past him.

Almost afraid to find out what had caught her attention, he turned. The MacBride brothers sat in heated debate over a handheld videogame. On the table in front of Matt, a shower of white crystals dusted the surface all around his mug. Evidently, one of the boys had managed to steal time away from the entertainment long enough to add salt to his root beer.

He looked back at Kerry. "Which one did it?"

"Uh-uh, Counselor." She raised her hands, palms out. "You're not pulling me in as a witness. I didn't see a thing."

"I'll bet." He pushed the mug away from him, scraping a path through the salt. "You MacBrides all hang together."

She moved toward him, frowning, and muttered, "That sounds like another one of your threats."

"No. Only my trained eye making an observation."

"Very funny."

He leaned down, copying her move, getting closer.

"What are you doing?" she asked.

He chuckled. "Getting an awareness of my surroundings."

Judging by that telltale flush on her cheeks, she was already very keenly aware—of him.

He could easily return the favor.

In fact, he'd been unable to get his mind off her ever since he'd been crazy enough to kiss her. On the one hand, he'd thoroughly enjoyed the experience. On the other, he wanted like hell to forget it. He'd never felt more confused in his life.

What had gotten into him, teasing her, kissing her—when he should just walk away?

KERRY SPENT AN UNEASY hour trying to distract Matt. Anything to keep him from an outright confrontation with any member of her family.

He spent half the time glowering toward one end of the table, where Uncle Bren kept Gran and Olivia laughing through their meal, and the other half of the time sneaking suspicious looks at the boys sitting at the opposite end.

In between, he managed to focus his attention on her, flirting with her and keeping her mind actively working at matching his quick wit. Though she enjoyed his teasing, she didn't trust it.

So she was more than ready to leave when everyone had finished eating.

"Kerry Anne," Gran said as they filed out of the packed restaurant into the cooler air outside, "what have you done about your car?"

"I called the shop this afternoon. It's ready for pickup. I'll go home tomorrow and get it on Monday."

"But you will be back again?" Gran asked.

"Yes." She was in this for the duration, now. No turning back, no hiding out at her studio at home, no hopping a plane for Europe. Right now, she had no time in her life for all those dreams. Plain and simple, she had to take care of her family.

"How will you get up to Chicago, love?" Gran's forehead puckered with worry. But her eyes were suspiciously bright.

"I'll drive her," Colin said instantly.

"Not a chance," Kerry told him. "You don't even have your permit yet."

"It'll be great practice for when I *do* get it."

"No, thank you."

"Uncle Bren can take you," Brody offered.

"That's what I was hoping." Smiling, she turned to her uncle. "We can leave first thing in the morning, and—"

"Uh, Kerry." He cleared his throat. "I would love to, but I've got plans for the car tomorrow. All day. If I could change them at this late notice, you know I would, but…"

"Matthew," Olivia spoke up. "Didn't you say you were getting an early start in the morning?"

"A very early start, Mom." His expression stayed neutral with what looked like an effort.

She didn't understand his reactions at all. *He'd* made the first move to kiss her out on the pier, not the other way around. Then, after they'd left the amusement park, he'd grown quiet, as if he didn't want to be in her presence. And yet, all during the meal, he'd flirted with her. Now, it seemed, he was back to avoidance.

She wished the man would just make up his mind!

Somehow, she managed to keep from saying her thoughts aloud. If he didn't want her company on the ride home, she wouldn't grovel.

"I'm sure Kerry wouldn't care about having to get up a little early," Olivia pressed.

Kerry could have sworn the gleam in her eyes matched Gran's. For crying out loud, were the two women keeping score?

Matt shook his head. "Kerry would mind, as early as I'm planning to leave."

Now he was making assumptions about her. Annoyance turned to irritation. "I'm up at 4:00 a.m. every school day," she said coolly, staring at him.

"That's the time I was intending to head out," he said, not looking at her. "All right, then, I'll pick you up in the morning."

"The problem is solved." Gran beamed and, taking Olivia's arm, began walking toward the parking lot.

Everyone else followed.

At the rear of the procession, Kerry swallowed hard and

turned in Matt's direction. "Thanks for letting me go along for the ride."

He shrugged. "I'm headed that way, anyhow."

"Oh." Well, she shouldn't feel let down about his response. After all, he hadn't agreed to take her home because he couldn't live without her company.

As a last resort, she could back down, could ask Uncle Bren to change his plans. But she really didn't want him making the long drive to Chicago and then the equally long trip back home.

She was stuck with Matt.

Or, judging by his attitude, he was stuck with her.

"Fine, then," she said politely. "I'll be outside Gran's at four." If her words were clipped, Matt didn't seem to notice.

Obviously, being this close to her family had cooled any interest he might have had where she was concerned.

The story of her life.

It was all for the best, of course—any relationship between them would be doomed. They could never survive as a couple. They hadn't even lasted through this weekend together.

The faint hopes she had built since that kiss they'd shared promptly collapsed.

DURING THE DRIVE BACK to Chicago the next morning, all Matt could think of was Kerry sitting beside him. Kerry teasing and taunting and drawing pictures of him. Kerry warm and comfortable in his arms.

He must have driven on autopilot, because he sure didn't remember making the trip back to Chicago.

By the time he pulled up to the curb in front of her apartment house, he felt as if he'd argued at the bench for hours—without having said a word.

She had read a book during the entire drive, which was fine with him. He hadn't had anything to say to her and didn't want anything else to do with her. Or her crazy family, who seemed to have successfully corrupted his mom, too.

He wondered where Kerry's parents were and why she and her brothers had lived at Lakeside Village with their grandparents. He thought about the phone call she'd received on their way out of town the other day and felt curious about the plans she'd given up to help her uncle. He wondered a lot of things about Kerry Anne MacBride.

But that didn't mean he wanted to be matched up with her.

When he had carried her bags inside and left her on the doorstep, he was determined to leave all thoughts of her behind.

He went home to his empty apartment and, for lack of anything better to do, raided the refrigerator. The hunk of dried cheese and the four-day-old container of take-out Chinese did nothing to distract him or make him feel better.

A few laps around the hoops might. He got into a T-shirt, shorts and athletic shoes and headed for the basketball court a few blocks from home.

On the way, he made a couple of stops, winding up in front of a newspaper kiosk where a withered old woman broke into a toothless smile when she saw him.

He'd once successfully defended Mary on a trumped-up loitering charge, and though he'd taken the case pro bono, she'd insisted on repaying him in the only way she could—with free newspapers. She'd have delivered them to his doorstep if she'd known where he lived. As it was, he made sure that every time he stopped by, he evened the score by bringing a cup of her favorite tea with honey. He plopped the covered paper cup on the counter and grinned back at her.

"Morning, Mary."

"What kind?" she asked shrewdly. "Good or bad? You're not saying?"

"Fair."

"Ahh. And just how'd that ride down south go?"

He shrugged, wishing now he hadn't decided to stop for a last-minute newspaper before picking up Kerry on Friday afternoon. Wishing twice as hard that he hadn't told Mary briefly about the situation in Lakeside.

"Cat got your tongue, huh? That's a bad sign. Or a good one, depending which way you look at it." She winked. "So tell me about it, Mr. Lawrence."

"Nothing to tell." He considered—for the hundredth time—all the reasons he needed to stay away from Kerry MacBride. "She's not my type at all. I don't like petite women. And you know I prefer blondes." He pretended to leer at her.

Ninety if she was a day, Mary still got a kick out of flirting.

She cackled and patted her faded hair. "The best butter don't get you more than a newspaper, and you know it. Besides, I asked about the trip, not the lady you took along with you. Guess that means she made an impression."

She'd caught him there. Running his thumb over his eyebrow, he laughed sheepishly. "Yeah, Mary. A *bad* impression. She's too outspoken, like someone else I know. And independent."

"That ought to go down fine with you. You're not one to like clinging vines."

He shook his head. "Independence is fine, commendable even, but she's too bossy along with it. Too ready to light into people and take them down a few notches. And she's got way too many relatives."

"Those are all good things! You need a woman like that, somebody to get you out of yourself. Somebody with good genes in the family so you can finally get some little ones of your own."

"Mary…" He knew his warning tone wouldn't deter her.

She spent her spare time trying to pair him up with every woman minus an engagement or wedding ring who stopped by her kiosk.

"What's she look like?" she asked, quickly changing the subject.

"Petite, as I said." He thought about Kerry, barely reaching his chin. But not lacking inches in all the right places. "Blue eyes. Red hair."

"Ahh. Got a temper?"

"Oh, yeah."

"A real feisty one, I'll betcha."

He nodded, calm on the outside but fighting a whirlwind of thoughts inside. With that one word—*feisty*—he was immediately back where he started. Thinking of Kerry.

Dry-mouthed and swallowing hard, he pushed aside the paper Mary had left on the counter. "Hang on to it," he croaked. "I'll pick it up after my run." He waved and walked away, trying to forget the knowing look she had given him.

A block away, he cut across the ring of bare earth circling the basketball hoops and tossed his towel onto a bench, then did a few minutes' worth of warm-ups before his first lap.

He could have afforded a membership at any of Chicago's priciest gyms, but he preferred to come to this beaten track of earth. It kept him closer to his childhood, in touch with the days he didn't want to remember but couldn't let himself forget.

Kerry had gotten it completely wrong when she'd accused him of having all the advantages. You didn't get many of those when you grew up with a single mom. When money was tight and time together even tighter. When you had to fight your way through a tough neighborhood to get to school every day.

No wonder he never wanted to visit the rundown areas of

town, like the one Kerry had taken him to the other day in search of her student J.J.

He pushed himself to run another lap, tried to clear his mind, to think of nothing, or at least of things that didn't raise his blood pressure or set off cravings for Kerry.

Instead, he thought of her all the more.

Her evasiveness bothered him. Her refusal to answer his questions irritated him, as well. But despite his suspicions, no matter how he tried, he couldn't get her out of his mind.

And that wasn't good at all.

He wanted to find the right woman, someday. Wanted a family of his own—but on his terms. His way. A stable, secure, *sane* family, made up of two loving parents and a few energetic but well-behaved kids.

If he ever settled down, it wouldn't be with a woman like Kerry MacBride.

And it sure wouldn't be with one who had a crazy family like hers.

He ate up the dusty track with furious speed, pushing himself into extra laps and hoping exhaustion would set in. Soon.

Back at the bench, he grabbed his towel and rubbed down, wishing he could scrub his thoughts away as easily.

It wasn't just Kerry he needed to get away from, it was those uncontrollable kids, that conniving grandmother and, most of all, that scheming uncle of hers.

He'd left them all behind, had washed his hands of the last of them when he'd finally deposited Kerry on her doorstep.

Now, when he went back to Lakeside again, he could focus on what really mattered. Taking care of his own family.

Whether his mom wanted him to or not.

Chapter Ten

As soon as she was able to pick up her car on Monday morning, Kerry headed to Lakeside. In the early afternoon, her band of volunteers gathered at the Village's game room for a short planning meeting, then proceeded to the old amusement park.

After a few minutes to catch up on her notes, Kerry followed.

The sun shone brightly, and a light breeze stirred the wildflowers lining the path that circled the lake. She turned her feet firmly toward the dirt pathway.

If only she could turn her thoughts as firmly away from Matt.

The ride home to Chicago yesterday morning had taken less time than she'd anticipated. Matt had stayed quiet, barely speaking to her during the entire trip. Even so, the air between them seemed to crackle with thoughts unspoken, emotions held in check, memories of their kiss.

Afraid to trust her subconscious with her sketchpad, she buried her nose in a book she'd borrowed from Gran. Though it was written by one of their favorite authors, with a forensic pathologist main character and a serial killer on the loose, the book couldn't keep her attention. Still, holding it allowed her to pretend she wasn't aware of every move Matt made.

He dropped her off at home, insisted upon opening her

car door and helping her with her bags as far as the front of the house. Then, after a short but awkward silence, he smiled politely, said goodbye and left her alone on the step.

Why that had bothered her, she didn't know.

Why that *continued* to bother her this Monday afternoon, she was sure she knew but definitely didn't want to think about.

She had more pressing problems at hand. And J .J. Grogan was one of them.

She had stopped by his house again on the way out of town. His mother's boyfriend, Hector, wasn't there, thank goodness. But neither was J.J. His mother said she hadn't seen him for days.

"He's a big boy now, does what he wants, I can't control him," she whined.

Knowing the woman's frustration came more from her home life—such as it was, with Hector around—than it did from her son, Kerry had bitten her tongue. But now her own frustration boiled over with worry about J.J.

She increased her pace, as if she could run away from *all* the thoughts that concerned her today, and soon reached the amusement park.

As she approached the entrance, she saw a figure leaning up against the archway, one boot-shod foot braced against the support, his arms crossed, his head turned away. At the sound of her footsteps on the wooden pier, he shifted to look in her direction.

She blinked, sure the sun had dazzled her. Sure she'd suffered heatstroke from her rapid trip around the lake. Sure her eyes had tricked her into seeing someone that wasn't really there.

But he *was* there.

And when Matt gave her a lopsided grin, her heart gave a little jolt that left it feeling lopsided, too.

"What are you doing here?" she asked. Much as she wanted to believe he'd come back to Lakeside for her, she realized the impossibility of that.

"I decided it would be in everyone's best interest if I stuck around."

He meant his mother and the other residents connected to the amusement park, of course. "Your mom must have been glad to see you again."

"She hasn't yet. I dropped my stuff off at the local motel, but I need to break that to her gently."

She frowned, puzzled.

"It's her furniture," he explained. "The only couch she's got is a couple of feet too short for me. It's fine for a night or two, but after that, I'm out of there." He tilted his head from side to side, stretching his neck. "I still haven't gotten rid of the kinks from the weekend." Then he smiled. "You could offer me a bed at your gran's place."

She froze. He was at it again, teasing her. Or could he possibly be serious?

It didn't matter. Just the idea of sharing a house with him made her hot all over. At the same time, the thought of sharing a house with him *and her family* gave her chills. She couldn't handle either response. "Sorry," she said shortly. "We haven't even got floor space to spare."

"Yeah, with that brood I can see why. How did you all ever live together in that little house?"

"It wasn't easy. But my two older brothers were already on their own, and the rest of us made do. I got the couch—and it was plenty long enough for me."

"I'll bet." His eyes met hers. Then, he dropped his gaze, looked slowly down the length of her.

He began it as a teasing gesture, she was sure. She could almost see the smart remark about her height forming on his lips. But by the time he made his way even more slowly up her body again, his expression told her it had turned into something more.

And that couldn't happen.

Unwillingly, she stumbled back a half step, taking her away from him, breaking the connection that seemed to have developed between them. She had a good imagination, but there was no sense letting it run wild here. Or anywhere. Ever.

"You couldn't have taken one more night on your mom's couch?" she asked, desperate for something to say.

"It'll be more than a night. As of today, I'm on vacation."

"You're *what?*" Everything around her shifted out of place, like the kaleidoscope she used during class to teach her students about patterns. She gulped, took a second, calmer breath, and said, "But—you're a lawyer. Don't you have cases to handle?"

"I have a secretary, clerks and paralegals to take care of some of the paperwork and research. But there's nothing pressing at the moment. Anyhow, lawyers get time off, too, you know."

"Not for good behavior, I'll bet." She started along the pier.

"I figure you need me on the team."

That stopped her midstride. "You're joking. Aren't you?" Saturday had been bad enough. She didn't need endless days with Matt at her heels.

"Do I look like I'm joking?"

"Unfortunately, no." She swallowed hard. "Well, thanks for the offer, but it's not necessary."

"But I insist." When she opened her mouth to protest, he continued, "The clock's ticking, Kerry. Face it, there's a lot that needs to get done around here. A heck of a lot. We saw that the other day. And you need all the help you can get."

"We'll manage."

"Kerry." He stared her down. "I'm not going anywhere."

His hazel eyes had turned emerald-green today, picking up the color of his T-shirt. She looked longingly into their depths for just another second, then steeled herself. "All right," she said finally. "I suppose knowing where you are will be better than not having a clue what you're up to."

He grinned, jolting her heart again. "What's the game plan?"

"I need to take a look behind the scenes. You know, check out a few off-limits areas, crawl under the roller coaster. That kind of thing."

It wasn't true. Carl, the retired engineer, would take on that job and get a certified engineer to back him up. But she hoped the idea alone would make Matt get lost in a hurry.

Deliberately, she took a turn looking him over, beginning at those annoying mirrored sunglasses and the hundred-dollar haircut, continuing along his spotless clothing, ending at his polished boots. "A dirty job, but somebody's got to get filthy doing it."

"Bring it on," he said, shoving the glasses up the bridge of his nose, then hooking his thumbs in his belt loops like some urban cowboy missing his six-shooters.

Dismayed, she turned away. Obviously, she couldn't shake this man from her trail as easily as she had anticipated. That didn't mean she'd give up trying. Eventually she would succeed.

Shaking his opinion of Uncle Bren and the entire amusement park project was another story altogether.

MATT WATCHED AS KERRY disappeared into the first wooden booth, a small shack with a waist-high counter running around three sides and a full wall at the rear.

He looked along the length of the pier. At the opposite end, the Ferris wheel towered over everything, looking faded and faraway and about ready to topple into the lake. Might be the best thing that could happen. If he stumbled across *any* evidence proving this pier was unsafe and this entire project was a farce, no one could argue with him about closing this park.

Not even Kerry.

She appeared at the front counter of the nearby booth.

He crossed the space, leaned casually toward her, watched her cheeks turn pink. "Looks like you're ready to run the whole show."

He smiled, but with mixed emotions. Seeing her again had made him happier than it should have. At the same time, it made him afraid. Very afraid.

For some reason, teasing Kerry had become complicated, both more fun than he'd expected and more hazardous than he liked. He wanted to see that flush cross her cheeks and that confused look touch her eyes. Both proved she was as unsettled by him as he was by her.

He was playing a dangerous game here, without a doubt. But the stakes—in terms of his mother's life savings—far outweighed the risk.

Still, feeling rattled, he looked away and gestured at a row of buttons on the counter between them. "What's this supposed to be?"

Her brows lowered in puzzlement. "Don't you know?"

"Would I be asking?"

"It's a wheel of chance." She pointed to one end of the counter near him, where a round, flat disk had been attached to the upright beam supporting that corner of the shack. Wooden pegs edged the disk at right angles, and a long metal piece like the hand of a clock spanned the face of it.

"How does it operate?" he asked.

"You push a button to spin the metal hand in the middle." She reached beneath the counter, fumbled with something, then frowned and tried again. "It's not working."

"And that surprises you?"

She glared at him. "No, not a bit. I'd forgotten it runs on electricity, and naturally, the power's out. I'm getting that taken care of. Anyhow, when the spinner stops between two of the pegs, it's hovering over a picture. If someone has a marker on that picture, they've won that prize."

Matt reached up and brushed a finger against the metal hand, trying to turn it manually. It didn't move. "Probably rusted beyond hope," he told her.

"Probably just needs some oil," she shot back.

This time, he added pressure with his finger. The metal gave a loud, squeaking groan and began to move. "And this is supposed to win a prize?"

"Yes." Her brows went down again. "Haven't you ever played the wheel at an amusement park or carnival?"

"Never been to either one."

"Never?" She sounded shocked beyond belief.

"It's kid stuff, Kerry Anne."

Crossing his arms, he leaned on the counter, bringing himself closer to her. He could see the muscles in her throat working as she tried to swallow.

"You must have been a kid, once," she said, her voice cracking. "There isn't any other option."

He grinned. "Doesn't matter. Neither of us are kids any more. So, now you're a grown-up, what would you like to win?"

She blinked.

Her ever-present clipboard wavered in front of his eyes. The damned thing gave her protection, made a physical barrier between them, and now, even gave her an excuse to look away.

She made a note on the top sheet, frowned down at it, and said, "I don't play games of chance."

"But you do play other games?"

"No." She looked him in the eye. "I don't play games. I don't pull tricks. And I don't run scams."

She backed away from him and went through the opening in the rear wall. Feeling no guilt, he waited for her to reappear.

She might be innocent of any trick when it came to this project. Regardless, she'd gotten her proposal passed behind his back and she continued to support the person who *had* perpetrated a scam.

Abruptly, she marched out from behind the booth and, without looking back, strode toward the next one on the pier.

He frowned. Logic told him it would definitely be safer for him to keep his distance. But not nearly as much fun.

He headed after her.

They moved from stand to stand, from something she called a ringtoss to another game that involved catching wooden goldfish to a booth he could finally recognize, a shooting range.

At this stand, a row of weather-worn plastic shotguns lined the counter. At one or two stations, a broken support pin showed where a gun had once been and had gone missing.

"You'll need to replace these," he said, indicating the empty pins.

"We'll need to replace all of them," she said, making a note on her clipboard.

"Looks like the targets have had it, too." He pointed to a couple of rusted silhouettes near the back wall.

"I've about had it myself," she said through clenched teeth. "Why are you doing this? Why are you bothering to point out all that's wrong about everything?" He could see the effort it took for her to put the clipboard down lightly on the countertop. "Matt, I'm as aware as you are that a lot of work needs to be done around here. That's why I'm taking inventory."

Now a pang of guilt did strike him, but it came and left in a moment. *Life savings are at stake.* "Look, we're both caught in the crossfire of this situation. I'm sorry about that, but it's your uncle's doing, not mine. So don't try putting the blame on me."

"Then don't go putting pressure on me." She stared him down. "You promised me sixty days. You can't expect me to have everything in order in the blink of an eye."

It wasn't getting things "in order" that mattered. It was getting money back to its rightful owners. He had to keep that in mind, and not be distracted by cute-and-beautiful Kerry MacBride.

As the silence went on between them, she blinked and ran a hand through her hair, dislodging the crossed pencils she'd had stuck behind her head. A few long curls fell, dangling near her face, looking soft and sexy and touchable.

As unlike the woman herself right now as they could be.

Turning, she strode off, her loose curls dancing like flames.

He stared after her, enjoying the fire. He wanted to pull those pencils from her hair. He wanted to let *all* those curls hang free. He wanted…to bring his wandering thoughts back to the business at hand. They refused to cooperate.

A long sigh shuddered through him.

Why was he struggling over this?

He'd come to his decision before leaving Chicago, had returned to Lakeside firmly intending to keep the promises he'd made to himself: He would talk to Kerry, but not touch her. Tease her, flirt with her, but not get involved.

Obviously, his brain and body didn't want to obey.

They would have to. But could they?

Hadn't they already let him down?

The realization hit with the stunning force of a riot baton.

No matter his decisions, his honorable intentions, his need to make things right for his mom once in his life, he had to admit the truth to himself. And only to himself.

He'd come back to Lakeside—back to Rainbow's End—because he'd had to.

Because he couldn't stay away.

A SHORT WHILE LATER, Kerry heard the sounds of sneakers slapping heavily against the wooden planks of the pier and sighed in relief. Anything to get a break from Matt, who had been shadowing her every move.

"Hey! What're ya doin'?"

She turned to see Brody racing toward them, flapping his arms and legs in exaggerated motion.

Colin followed at a more deliberate pace.

She had to swallow a smile. Her brothers would be sure to rub Matt the wrong way, but that could be all to the good. The tension between them seemed almost tangible.

They needed something else to focus on besides each other.

Brody's childish antics would do it.

"We're taking inventory," she answered him.

"Taking it where?"

Colin rolled his eyes.

Before Kerry could answer, Brody's attention snapped to Matt. "Hey, I'm gonna be a juggler in the circus, did I tell you?" He pulled out the three worn rubber balls he was never without and began bouncing them from hand to hand.

"You did mention it," Matt said.

"Yeah. A juggler—and a lion tamer."

"You've had a lot of experience training wild animals, have you?"

"Only Blank."

"And that would be…"

"Gran's cat," he explained. "Blanketyblank. She's pretty wild—but only when you're pulling her tail."

"Do you do that often?" Matt's lips compressed, as if he were holding back a laugh.

"If Gran's not around, sure. It's fun." Brody squinted up at him. "I was gonna run away and join the circus right now, but Kerry said I have to wait till I'm eighteen." He scowled. "Then I'll be too old to have *any* fun."

"I doubt that," Matt said. "You can still find things to amuse you when you get to that age—and even older." He turned to Colin. "What are you going to do at this circus? Be the ringleader?"

Colin snorted. "Ha-ha. Real funny. I'm going to be a mountain climber."

"Wanna see me?" Brody interrupted, hopping from foot to foot. "Hey, look!"

They watched as he tossed the balls a little higher, moved them more rapidly from hand to hand. With all the practice he got in, he actually had become fairly skillful at juggling the soft rubber balls.

"Not bad," Matt said, nodding.

"Anybody can do that," Colin said scathingly.

Brody grabbed the balls in midair and glared at him. "Oh, yeah? Let's just see *you* do it."

Colin said nothing.

"I'll show *you*." Brody moved across to the side of the pier and hoisted himself onto the wooden railing.

"Brody—" Kerry began.

"I got it, Ker." He planted his feet and rose to stand upright on the rail. "It's easy. See?" He tossed one ball after another, until he again had all three in play. The bright rubber flashed in the sun as he bounced the balls from hand to hand. "Told ya I'd show you, Col," he boasted.

"What's so hot about that?"

"Colin…" This had gone too far, in Kerry's opinion.

What would Matt be thinking of the boys? They were so rowdy and energetic, and he was… He was a lawyer. A serious, straitlaced, by-the-book lawyer.

And how would he connect their actions to *her?* She hadn't thought about that when she'd welcomed her brothers as a distraction.

"Colin," she finished, "that's enough. And, Brody, that's dangerous. Get down—"

"I bet *you* can't do—" Brody lost his footing. His words ended in a shriek. He flailed his arms, trying to stay on the rail.

All three of them jumped to his aid.

All three of them were just a second too late.

Brody plunged from the pier and landed with a tremendous splash in the lake.

Chapter Eleven

Matt strode down the hallway of the clubhouse, thinking of Brody MacBride and shaking his head.

They'd gotten the kid out without having to drag the lake. He'd swum over to one of the pilings and raised both hands—the balls clutched in his dripping fingers—high enough for Matt, spread-eagled on his stomach on the wooden boards, to reach down and haul him up.

Brody had turned out none the worse for wear and water—until he discovered he'd lost the third rubber ball and screeched twice as loudly as when he'd fallen into the lake.

Kerry, looking more dismayed than either of the boys, had sent them home.

Somehow, Matt managed to get through the rest of the afternoon without commenting on her crazy brothers.

He also managed to survive not getting close enough to touch Kerry.

All right—to tell the truth, she was such a whirlwind of activity, he had trouble keeping up with her. But he'd made a vow to keep her in sight at all times.

If this situation could have been handled in a logical way, he would never have needed to take vacation time. He could have contacted his mother frequently by phone.

He could have gotten updates from Kerry long-distance. But could he trust her for those updates? Not a chance.

She hadn't given him satisfactory replies about her uncle the other day, and that fact still bothered him. Well, when the detective he'd contacted came through, he'd find out all there was to discover about Brendan MacBride.

Kerry was another story.

He didn't like the fact that she evaded his questions. Or the habit she had of walking off and leaving him more uncertain than before. She was quick on her feet and she was smart; he'd recognized that from their very first meeting. The only solution to keep her from getting away was to stay right by her side.

He nodded in satisfaction at the idea. From now on, Kerry Anne MacBride would be sharing more than conversation with him.

She'd be sharing her personal space. On a regular basis.

They'd just returned from an early dinner, and he'd taken a trip to the clubhouse office to pick up yet another package that had been delivered for the amusement park. He walked into the game room now to find her alone, her cell phone at her ear.

"I'm sorry, too, Professor." Her voice cracked. "You know how much it meant to me. I'd give anything to get on the next plane, but I can't leave my family right now."

He paused in the doorway, about to retreat into the hall. Her back was to him, and she didn't know he was listening. This seemed like it could be the same professor she'd talked to the other day during their ride to Lakeside. She wouldn't discuss that call with him then and probably wouldn't discuss this one now. He wondered what was up. Sooner or later, he'd find out.

Before he could move, she said into the cell phone, "All right. Please let them know how sorry I am. And have a wonderful summer." She clicked off the phone, set it down on the nearby pool table in front of her and picked up her clipboard. Her shoulders slumped, as if she held an enormous weight.

After clearing his throat to announce his presence, he walked up and plopped the box on the table. "Here it is."

He watched her enter the new arrival on her board, then go down the list, checking off the items they needed to transfer to the only fully enclosed building on the pier.

Her face was like a mask, without expression or emotion. That bothered him. He had to say something that would get a response.

"You're very orderly for an artist, aren't you?" he asked.

She looked over at him and frowned. "Well, thanks for the backhanded compliment."

"No problem. But I didn't intend it that way. I'm impressed by your organization. I mean that sincerely."

"Thanks." This time, the words came with a small smile.

"It's too bad you're not getting more help. You've got to admit, we haven't seen much of the other MacBride adults around here." He considered himself a candidate for sainthood for not pointing out they hadn't seen her uncle at all.

"And we've had too much contact with the younger MacBrides," she put in. "Is that what you're saying?"

He looked her straight in the eye. "Do you expect me to argue that?"

"I suppose not." She gave a half-strangled laugh. "Not after Brody's big splash."

"A big responsibility for you, taking care of those boys."

"Gran does most of it."

The easy conversation between them made him think he could risk trying to find out more about her. "You're very... levelheaded compared to the rest of your family. Who do you take after? Your mom?"

"I hope not!"

He stared in surprise at the heat in her voice. "I gather you aren't on good terms."

"Our letters were friendly enough."

He raised inquiring eyebrows.

She shrugged. "She and my father were archeologists. They were always away on digs, or at conferences or off drumming up finances to support their trips overseas. So we wrote to each other. Occasionally." She smiled, but he didn't see any happiness in it. "It was like having a pen pal who'd drop me a line from time to time."

"That must have been devastating."

"I got a great stamp collection out of it." This time, she tried a laugh. It broke in the middle.

"Don't you see them at all?"

"I did, once in a while, when they were between projects or needed to do their fundraising in this part of the country. Or when my mother came back home to have another baby."

"They ought to be brought up on abandonment charges." He tried to temper his words, to make his tone more sympathetic, but couldn't do it. The raw pain in her expression caused him to champion her, the same way he defended his clients in court. "They sound awful."

She shook her head. "They weren't, really. Actually, they were wonderful, fun and full of life and exciting to be around. And very much in love with each other. They just weren't cut out to be parents." With her free hand, she waved as if to erase her last statement. "Maybe that's too cruel. Maybe they just didn't have the kind of job that made it easy to stay together as a family."

"Yet they didn't mind having a brood of kids and leaving them with your dad's parents to raise."

"I don't know." She turned back to her clipboard and sighed. "Things might have been different if they hadn't been killed in an accident a few years ago."

His breath caught at the flat, matter-of-fact statement, and he waited for her to explain. But she simply continued with her thought.

"Eventually, they might have retired and come home to raise us. Or Colin and Brody, at least."

He wanted the rest of the story but knew the value of letting a witness lead.

"Instead, Gran and Grandpa raised us."

"They just took their son's kids in, enabling your parents to go on their way, letting them shirk their responsibilities."

"If they hadn't, my parents would have left us with someone else."

"You don't mean that."

"Yes, I do."

The skin around her eyes looked strained and pale. He suddenly realized that pushing her to talk made him no better than her parents. Damn his inquisitive nature.

"Archeology was their life." She sighed. "My family tends to run to obsessions. Gran and her environmental issues. My parents and their archaeology. Gran found room in her house and her life—and her heart—to take us all in. For my parents, the archaeology was enough. They had that—and each other. They didn't need anyone or anything else."

He shook his head. He'd seen plenty of kids involved in worse situations. He hadn't had it much better himself, if he got right down to it. In fact, things had actually gotten better once he'd had an absentee parent. But Kerry's situation, and her reaction to it, tugged at emotions he didn't know he had.

"I'll confess," she said, looking back at him, "I'm envious of your relationship with your mom. You obviously love each other and get along well."

"We do. We always have. And she knows how much I look out for her interests."

"I'm sure she does. Even I can see that." She paused, then added, "What about your father? You've never said anything about him."

He shifted away from her, shuffled his feet, cleared his throat. He didn't want to talk about the man, didn't even want to think about him.

"Hey." He attempted a grin and knew he'd failed. "How'd we get so serious all of a sudden? And why all this talk about the past? We've got enough going on in the present."

"But most of it's not something we can discuss. At least, not without arguing over it."

Her mouth twisted in what had probably started out as a smile. He didn't like the expression at all. He wanted to see her lips smooth again, wanted to feel her mouth under his. Wanted her to smile, fully and genuinely, showing off that cute crooked-tooth grin. All for him.

A shiver went through him. Lust? Fear? Anticipation?

Maybe all of the above.

He lunged for the package they had picked up from the hardware store when they'd gone out for their supper. "I'd better run this lock over to Carl, if you're still planning to move these supplies to the pier today."

She nodded and turned back to her job. He took one last, lingering look at her before turning away and running the back of his hand across his suddenly damp forehead.

It had occurred to him there was one thing they could do that they didn't have to argue about.

And it didn't involve talking at all.

"Whew. Well, that's done." Kerry sighed and wiped her forearm across her forehead. "It's very late—all that took a lot longer than I'd expected."

With Colin and Brody's version of assistance, they had finally carted all of the supplies from the game room over to the storage shed. Then she had sent the boys home before meticulously going through her inventory sheets again. Not that she didn't trust her brothers. But she had to admit they were a handful with all their shenanigans. Better to make sure everything tallied, because it would be just her bad luck to have the man standing beside her discover something missing.

She looked at Matt, who had spoken very little during this last job of the day. The presence of the boys, energetic as they were, might have had something to do with that.

"It's been a long day," she said, unable to come up with anything more interesting. Too bad she hadn't resorted to trite phrases earlier, instead of so uncharacteristically dumping her life history on him. She never opened up to anyone about her family—and she still regretted telling him as much as she had. "We've inventoried every single item now on this pier."

"Twice, I think."

She couldn't hold back a laugh. "Well, we had the time, thanks to all the volunteers who handled the prep for the painting marathon tomorrow." Until Carl had finished inspecting all the equipment, they would concentrate on desperately needed cosmetic improvements to the park. She flipped the pages on her clipboard forward and shoved the pen into her hair. "I think we're done for the night."

Stepping past Matt, she exited the shed ahead of him. She'd had the electricity turned on, and after he'd followed her out, he flipped the switch and closed the door behind them.

Twilight had brought the twinkling lights of fireflies and the faint glow of a moon shadowed now and then by clouds. The air was warm and close.

And so was Matt.

Beside her, he secured the new padlock on the door. In the shadow of the building, she could barely see his eyes, but couldn't miss the silhouette of his strong jaw, firm mouth, stubborn chin.

A definite attraction. And a definite *dis*traction.

His presence beside her the entire afternoon and evening had made concentrating on her jobs a challenge.

After their initial skirmish that day over his joining the team, he'd proved himself an excellent worker, as well as a true gentleman. He'd politely held doors and escorted her in and out of buildings and booths, allowing her to enter first except when they'd come across any potentially hazardous situations. They had fallen into a reluctant but successful relationship. Truthfully, after their rocky start, his cooperation had surprised her.

"Thanks for your help today," she said softly.

"I'm on the team," he replied.

"Yes. So you are." *A reluctant but successful* working *relationship.* How foolish was she for wishing it could go beyond that? "I'll check the game room again in the morning," she said, half to herself, "just to make sure nothing was left behind."

"I doubt it." Matt leaned back against the door. "The way you had those volunteers hopping, they wouldn't dare miss anything."

"Am I that bad?" she asked in dismay.

"No, you're that good." He lightly touched one of the tendrils of hair that had fallen loose from her knot and rested against her shoulder. He lifted his hand, grazing his fingertips along the pulse at her neck. She felt the beat rise at his touch and hoped he hadn't noticed it, too.

He smiled down at her, as if he *had* noticed. As if he knew what she'd been thinking. Her breath caught in her throat.

He reached out for her, urging her closer to him.

She moved forward, tilted her head back, looked into his eyes, silvery in the light now that another cloud hovered in front of the moon.

He ran his hands slowly up her arms and across her

shoulders, finally curving his fingers around her face. His thumb brushed her mouth, and something trembled deep within her.

She closed her eyes and swallowed hard, her throat suddenly tight but the rest of her astonishingly relaxed, languid. Ready.

She could feel him move closer, could sense his breath on her lips. Then she heard a muttered curse and her eyes flew open.

"Damn it, Kerry." He laughed and shook his head. "You and this danged clipboard."

She looked down, surprised to find she still held it cradled against her.

He took the board from her nerveless fingers and dropped it to the wooden planks beneath their feet. "Let's try that again."

This time, he held her loosely in the circle of his arms.

He tilted his head down, she lifted hers, and they met somewhere in the middle.

This was wrong. Oh, not the kiss, but the entire situation. Them. Here. Together.

There was no future in a relationship with Matt.

Because of that, she would need these memories of him to look back on when he was gone.

She closed her eyes, letting the rest of her senses take over.

He tasted like the peppermint candy she'd given him after dinner. Smelled like a mixture of musk and spices. And felt—when she got up the nerve to spread her now empty hands against his chest—rock-solid. Reliable. As sturdy and as safe as the pier beneath their feet.

Her pulse raced, her heart sang, and the sound of bells chimed in her ears. Just like she'd seen in the movies.

So she was doubly startled when Matt suddenly lifted his head, breaking their kiss, and pushed her aside gently.

"Wh-what is it?" she murmured.

"I heard something fall, then footsteps. Someone's out here."

She frowned. "Who would be roaming around on the pier at this hour?"

"That's what I'm about to find out."

He moved quickly past her. She turned to follow but had forgotten about the clipboard. It caught beneath her foot, sliding out from under her. She went with it, landing hard on one knee and bracing her hand against the pier to stop her fall.

Stunned for a second, she froze in place.

Then she heard a thump followed by a deep-voiced yell, and in the space of a heartbeat she was on her feet again and running in the direction of the uproar.

Chapter Twelve

"No!" Kerry yelled, shocked at the sight near the park's ticket booth. A bewildered-looking Matt faced another man who stood with his shoulders hunched and his fists high. *"J.J.!"*

It was almost completely dark, but the bright moonlight and the fact that they'd been out here in the gloom for a while had allowed her eyes to adjust to the night. Still, she could barely believe what she was seeing.

Even from behind, one look at the tall, lanky frame and backward baseball cap told her it was J. J. Grogan. His protective stance made her heart go out to him.

When he whirled to face her, the sight of the puffy, discolored bruise swelling his left eye almost shut sent her heart to her throat.

"Ms. MacBride!"

She gasped, looked at Matt, then back at J.J. "What happened to you?"

He straightened to full height again and shrugged. "It's nothing, Ms. MacBride."

"It's *not* nothing, J.J. Who did that to you?"

He didn't say a word.

"It was Hector, wasn't it?" she pressed.

"Let it go, okay?" He shoved his hands in his back pockets. "Nothin' you can do about it, and things would only get worse, anyway. I didn't come here for that."

Reluctantly, she let the subject drop. For now. Maybe he didn't want to discuss it in front of Matt, who stood looking from one to the other of them in barely disguised surprise.

"How did you get here?" she asked.

"Hitched."

"J.J, that's so dangerous—"

"More to the point," Matt broke in, "*what* are you doing here?"

J.J eyed him for a second.

"I'm wondering, too," she told him.

He looked at her, then stared out over the lake and sighed. "Mom and Hector were fighting—"

"He hit you?" Matt demanded. "Did he hit your mother, too?"

"No." J.J. shrugged. "He doesn't hit, he only yells. He was throwing a beer bottle, and I got in the way."

"And what brought you here?"

Kerry rested her hand on Matt's arm. "How did you find me, J.J.?"

"I remembered your granny lived in Lakeside." He started to grin, then winced, probably from the pain of his swollen eye. "When I saw the Ferris wheel from the highway, I figured, can't be more than one amusement park in town. So this had to be it."

"That still doesn't tell us why you're here," Matt put in.

J.J. flicked his gaze toward him, but addressed his response to her. "I want to help with the park, Ms. MacBride. I want to work here for the summer."

"But…" There were so many reasons he shouldn't stay. She grabbed at the most relevant one. "J.J., I can't pay you."

"Don't matter. I've got some money. And I'll get a job, part-time, if I have to. Bagging groceries or something."

"Where are you going to sleep?" Matt asked.

J.J. shrugged. "I don't know. Maybe I can find a place

out here." He gestured around the pier. "Be like a night watchman."

"You can't just—"

"I don't think we need security," Kerry broke in. "We're not expecting any intruders. We didn't even expect you, did we, Matt?" She smiled, trying to ease the hostility between them.

"You can't live here," Matt said flatly. "In fact, if you don't want to be reported as a runaway, you'd better get on the next bus to Chicago."

"I'm not going back." His chin went up and he glared at Matt. "I'm eighteen. I can make my own decisions. And I want to stay."

His voice had risen a few notches. Not growing louder, but climbing to a higher, tighter pitch that told Kerry he was stressed to the breaking point and possibly frightened. Of the situation here or the one he had left, she didn't know. But maybe there was more to his story. Something he wouldn't discuss in front of a stranger.

She could see the panic in his face. She could also feel the tension radiating from Matt, standing stiffly beside her.

One of them would explode any minute.

"J.J., why don't you take a walk out by the parking lot? Give us a few minutes, okay?"

After a second, he nodded and moved away, stopping only to pick up a small duffel bag she hadn't noticed before. Then he trudged away from them.

They watched him move along the pier until he was swallowed up by the lengthening shadows.

She could see Matt's features dimly—and she had no problem at all picking up on the tension that still flowed from him as if in tangible waves.

"He's a good kid, Matt." And Matt was a good man. She knew it.

He stared off in the direction J.J. had gone. "This is the student you were talking about the other day, the one whose house we stopped by? The artist?"

"Yes."

"And I take it that was Hector, the mother's boyfriend, we ran into out there."

"Yes. He lives with them."

Finally, he looked at her. His eyes glinted in the moonlight. "The kid's got trouble."

"I know." She sighed. "I'd like to keep him away from it, at least long enough for me to find out exactly what's going on and how to handle it."

"You're letting him stay here?" he asked evenly.

"Well, not *here,* here. Not at the park. I told you, he's a good kid. A hard worker. I've known him through his four years of high school. He was once in a gang, but not anymore. He's starting college this fall, on a full, four-year scholarship. I'm so proud of him—and I trust him. Sleeping on the pier is no place for him. We'll work something out for tonight." She bit her lip, considering. They really couldn't fit another person in at Gran's.

J.J.'s reasons for coming here had to be substantial—and serious. She couldn't bear to just send him home again. But, no matter how much she vouched for him, what were the chances of anyone at Lakeside Village taking in an unknown teenager?

Unless…

"Matt." She cleared her throat. "You've already got a motel room for the night."

"Yes, I do. Are you propositioning me, Kerry Anne?"

Her cheeks flamed at the same time a nervous laugh escaped her. "Yes," she said positively.

His eyes widened, and his mouth stretched in a grin. But even as his deep chuckle rippled through her, threatening to send her thoughts in a different direction, she felt sure he knew what she intended.

He crossed his arms and gave her a straight-faced look. "This will take some serious argument," he said, confirming her suspicion.

"Fine." She took a deep breath. "Well, as I said, you've already got a motel room."

"Point taken."

"And it's already paid for."

"Yes."

"And I'm sure it's got two beds."

"Yes, as a matter of fact, it does." He leaned forward and murmured, "Maybe I had other ideas in mind than loaning one of them out to a teenage boy." He touched the loose curls at her shoulder.

"Maybe you did," she said, her voice cracking. She struggled to get control of it again. "But duty calls. You'll have to put those plans on hold."

"You'll have to make it worth my while," he countered.

She smiled slowly and reached up to run her hand through his hair, soft and thick beneath her fingertips. He leaned forward, and she gently pushed him away. "For that, Counselor, we'll need to meet in chambers."

"Yours or mine?" he asked.

She laughed. "At the moment, neither one's an option." She took a deep breath, let it out slowly. "You'd be willing, Matt?"

"Hell, I'm always willing."

"Come on, seriously. You'd be willing to put J.J. up?" Doubt crept into her voice. He couldn't want an unknown teenager around, either. But who else could she ask?

"No," Matt said flatly.

Her heart sank.

"But I'm not willing to tangle with your Irish temper,

either," he added. "And the motel's close enough, he can walk back and forth—if you really are going to let him work here."

She smiled. "As you said to me this afternoon, the clock's ticking, and I need all the help I can get."

"That's true enough."

"It's late now. But I *will* talk to him first thing tomorrow and see what the story is before I commit to anything but one night's stay."

"That's advisable. Then let's do it."

Before he could move away, she touched his arm. "Thank you, Matt. I really appreciate this."

"I wouldn't give out any thanks yet. As *you* said about *me* this afternoon, it's better to keep an eye on him than wonder what he's getting up to."

His words were harsh, but she caught the hint of humor in his tone. When he put his hand around hers and squeezed her fingers, she squeezed back. And when he turned, still holding on to her as he ambled toward the entrance of the amusement park and J.J., she twined her fingers through his and walked beside him.

She felt as happy and lighthearted as any of the love-struck teenagers at school.

The sound of their footsteps on the pier echoed over the lake. And words she didn't want to think about seemed to echo inside her mind.

Teenage romances usually come to heartbreaking endings.

OUTSIDE BILL'S RESTAURANT early the next morning, Matt cranked up the Jeep and headed in the direction of Lakeside Village.

In the seat beside him, J.J. leaned back and grinned. "Man, that was one good breakfast."

"Not bad, if you don't think about your cholesterol."

"Never happens," J.J. said airily.

Matt laughed.

Last night, they hadn't talked much, had just gone to the motel, washed up, turned in.

This morning, Matt deliberately took his time over his meal, trying to draw the boy out. Anybody who meant that much to Kerry had to be a good person. But anyone who could hurt Kerry also had to be checked out.

He and J.J. *did* have a good breakfast, in more ways than one. Matt had left the restaurant feeling he knew a lot about the boy.

"I see your eye's looking better this morning."

"Yeah." J.J. touched it with barely a wince. "Mr. Lawrence, y'know, when somebody shows up with a shiner, the joke is 'you oughta see the other guy,' right?"

"Right."

"Well, I want you to know I didn't touch him."

"That's a good thing, J.J. Retaliation doesn't get you anywhere." He drove for a couple of minutes in silence, then added in a neutral tone, "Hector hit you deliberately, didn't he?"

"He don't do anything deliberately," J.J. muttered. "He just sets up little 'accidents' that I walk into."

Of course. He wouldn't use his fists. Fists left marks.

Matt had learned that his first week in law school.

J.J.'s situation mirrored Matt's own as a kid in many ways.

His father hadn't used physical violence, either. And he hadn't been verbally abusive. Instead, he'd worked in just the opposite way—with words that drew people in. Manipulating his targets into giving him whatever he wanted. And, in the worst-case scenarios, making them feel it was what *they* had wanted all along.

"Ms. MacBride's the best," J.J. said suddenly, probably wanting to change the subject.

Matt jumped at the chance to get away from bad memories.

"In what way?" he asked, willing to go with the new topic, wanting to know more about the boy and genuinely curious as to why an eighteen-year-old would feel so strongly about a teacher.

"She just is." J.J. considered for a minute or two, then said, "First off, she's really into art."

"That makes her a good teacher?"

"Oh, yeah. If you don't get what she's saying, she can *show* you, which is the best, because art's visual, you know? You have to be able to see it."

"Mmm." Matt deliberately gave the low-key answer, hoping to lead J.J. on to more. The strategy worked.

"She helped turn lots of people around," J.J. added.

"How do you mean?"

"Just helping them. Get through school. Get off drugs."

"And staying away from gangs?" He glanced across the space in time to see J.J.'s shoulders go rigid.

"She told you about me?"

"Some," Matt said.

"Why?"

He looked the boy straight in the eye. "I was about to let you room with me. There were things she thought I should know."

Slowly, J.J. nodded agreement. "Those days are over, Mr. Lawrence."

Matt drove another minute in silence through Lakeside's small-town version of early-morning rush hour—two cars and a newspaper delivery van.

Could he trust J.J.'s truthfulness about his past?

So far, he hadn't seen any evidence to the contrary. In fact, he'd seen proof of Kerry's belief in the boy's honesty in the way she had taken him under her wing.

He glanced at J.J.

"I'm not involved with them anymore," the boy insisted, blinking but holding Matt's gaze.

Matt broke away first to return his attention to the road.

Blinking was good. It was the wide-eyed, don't-move-a-muscle stare you needed to watch out for. "So I hear. I also hear you were awarded a scholarship. I guess you're all geared up to go at the end of the summer."

"I...I don't know."

Matt pushed a button on the radio, changing the station, allowing the boy some psychological distance. He would talk more freely if he didn't think Matt was hanging on every word.

They'd arrived at his mother's apartment building. Matt turned into the visitor's parking area and pulled into a space.

J.J.'s silence stretched on. Matt turned off the Jeep and sat quietly, waiting.

Finally, J.J. blurted, "I need money, Mr. Lawrence. Lots of money."

Matt tensed. If J.J. had lied about his gang affiliation, or had gone into drugs, what would that do to Kerry's faith in her judgment?

Worse, as much as she cared about her students, especially J.J., what would that do to Kerry?

"It's my mom," J.J. burst out. "She's got to kick Hector out. She says she can't—he pays some of the bills. But if I get a full-time job, I can help her. She could get him out of the apartment. Out of our life."

Matt nodded. "You don't think Ms. MacBride has the right to know what's going on? Not to talk you into or out of anything. But I'm sure she did a lot to help you get where you are."

"She did. And I'm throwing it all away," he said bitterly.

"I'm not saying that, J.J. Just think about talking it over with Ms. MacBride, okay?"

"Okay."

"I'll be back in a couple minutes."

He left the Jeep and headed up the walk to his mom's apartment, mentally replaying the conversations he'd had with J.J. and not seeing a problem with any of them. Their talks had only confirmed what Kerry had told him—J.J. was a good kid.

And not only did he and J.J. have similar backgrounds, their situations now were even more alike than he had realized.

The boy wanted to help his mother.

How could Matt find fault in that?

MATT WENT UP THE APARTMENT stairs two at a time. He should have let his mom know yesterday that he was in town again. But once he'd seen Kerry, everything else had flown out of his head.

She had needed his help at the amusement park, whether she would admit it or not. He'd been right in saying they hadn't seen any of the adult MacBrides around. She'd been right when she'd come back with the remark about seeing too much of the younger ones.

He didn't think he'd ever get tired of looking at Kerry.

And that had almost led to disaster.

Last night, alone with her on the pier, he'd done a hell of a lot besides look—he'd touched and tasted and wanted more. Who knows what would have happened if J.J. hadn't shown up?

He'd owed that kid breakfast this morning.

Shaking his head, he came to a stop in front of his mom's

door and rang the bell. The echo had faded away inside the apartment before he heard footsteps tapping on the uncarpeted entryway. After another minute, the door opened, revealing his mom staring at him wide-eyed.

"Matthew! My goodness—I didn't expect you."

"I know. I would have called, but it was late when I got things settled."

"Is everything all right?" She pressed one hand against the edge of the door, lifted the other to her throat as if she'd lost her breath in surprise.

"Everything's fine." Seeing him seemed even more of a shock for her than he'd expected. He should have called first. "Do you think we could continue this conversation inside?"

"Of course." She opened the door wide and stepped back.

He entered, then froze in his tracks, staring over her shoulder.

Across her small living room in her even smaller dining area, looking guiltier than a bank teller with his hand in the till—and what an appropriate comparison *that* was—sat the last person he wanted to see.

Brendan MacBride.

No wonder Mom had looked so surprised.

"You've got company." He deliberately kept his tone flat.

"Come in, come in," MacBride said, as if he owned the place.

"A little early for a social call, isn't it?"

"Not social, lad. We're just discussing a few things about the park."

"That's right," his mom put in.

Matt took his time eyeing the table, its surface cluttered with coffee mugs, plates, sugar bowl and creamer. "Business breakfast, huh?"

"Absolutely." Grinning, MacBride rose, sidestepped around

the table and started across the room. "Always best to discuss business on a full stomach."

Exactly what Matt had often heard his father say.

He glared.

MacBride sidestepped again, this time around his mother, keeping her between them as he edged toward the door. "Well, I'll be off now, Olivia. Matthew, a pleasure to have you back again. I'm sure I'll see you over at the park."

"Will you? I was around yesterday and our paths didn't cross."

"Oh, but they will sure enough today. Kerry's got a painting party lined up for the lot of us. Work to be done, y'know."

"I know." That was all he said. It was enough.

MacBride nodded and slithered into the hall.

Matt would have looked out to make sure he'd really gone, but his mom's voice distracted him.

"You were here yesterday, Matthew, and didn't tell me?"

"Sorry. I would have called, but I got busy helping Kerry out at the pier, and then it was late."

"But where did you stay? With Kerry?"

He stared. She'd sounded pleased at the idea, and not a bit put out that he hadn't stayed with her. He shook his head again.

Everything in his life had gone wacky since he'd met the MacBride clan.

He told her about taking his vacation time *and* taking on a new roommate. "We're heading over now to start work."

"Good, then I'll see you later."

To his surprise, she practically pushed him through the doorway. She seemed in a hurry to get him to leave—and that wasn't like his mom at all.

It wasn't until he was outside again, climbing into the Jeep with J.J., that a possible reason for her actions struck him.

Maybe she wanted him out of the apartment because there

were other signs, along with the littered breakfast table-for-two, that she didn't want him to see.

WHEN MATT AND J.J. arrived at the pier, Matt looked twice as angry as Kerry had ever seen him.

"I'm going to walk off my breakfast," he muttered, then stalked away from them.

At least he'd delivered J.J. to her before leaving. She wondered what had gotten him so upset. She wondered if he planned to help out at the pier today.

"What's wrong, J.J.?"

He shrugged. "Don't know. He was fine till we stopped at his ma's. I waited outside. He was only in there five minutes."

She would have to worry about Matt later. Her volunteers would be showing up any minute, and she had to talk to J.J. He'd been adamant the night before about not going home. She needed to find out why.

When she questioned him, he seemed genuinely excited about the idea of helping to bring the old amusement park back to life. She wished she could have put some of that levelheaded enthusiasm into her brothers.

It didn't take her long to find out that, as she had thought, J.J. wanted some relief from his home situation. He assured her he hadn't been in touch with any of the members of the gang he'd once belonged to.

"Told you that the other day, Ms. MacBride. I just want to get away from Hector for a while." He kicked lightly at a cardboard carton. "You know, I try telling Ma he's no good, but she don't want to listen."

"I know, J.J. Some people need more time for a wake-up call, like the one you had about Benny and the guys." She paused, wanting to ask him about his plans for the future, about starting college in the fall. But until he straightened out his current situation, he probably couldn't look any further ahead than this.

"You're leaving on your trip soon, huh?" he said.

She hesitated, then admitted, "No. There have been some changes to my plans."

He stared at her.

"It's a long story, J.J." She sighed to herself, recalling her phone call yesterday. In one brief transatlantic call, she'd abandoned her fellowship, her trip to Europe and her hard-earned summer vacation. Today's painting marathon would probably be the closest she'd get to any artwork this summer. The worst of it was, this was all her own doing! "The amusement park took priority," she told him.

"I want to help, Ms. MacBride," J.J. said quietly, his voice strained. "You gonna let me stay?"

She noted his furrowed brow and clenched fingers. And couldn't miss the sight of his discolored, swollen eye. Thankfully, she saw it had improved considerably overnight.

"Yes," she said finally. "For now, anyway, and we'll see how it goes. But you have to promise me you'll call your mother and let her know where you are."

He nodded, a relieved grin lightening his worried expression.

She'd be talking to his mom, too.

"You want me to organize some of this stuff?" he asked eagerly, gesturing to the boxes stacked against the far wall.

"Yes, that's next on the agenda." She told him about relocating their "headquarters" to the storage room. Smiling, she thought of what he had interrupted when he'd arrived the night before. But she needed to stay focused. On J.J. "I wish you'd been here yesterday when we moved all these supplies over here."

"I'm here now."

"That you are." She hesitated again. Unable to keep her

thoughts from Matt, she added, "Everything go all right last night?"

"Yeah. We stopped at that Grill place this morning. Great food." His eyes widened at the memory.

She laughed. "Good. Then you're all fueled up to get to work—so get to it."

He raised his fingertips to his backward ball cap in a salute. "You got it." Immediately, he turned to his task.

If only all her problems could be handed off to someone else that easily.

Bracing herself, she took a long, deep breath. Then she headed out to search for Matt.

Chapter Thirteen

To Kerry's surprise, she found Matt wielding a paint scraper on one of the booths along the pier. At her approach, he looked up, then turned back. Funny, how *his* enthusiasm for work didn't please her as much as J.J.'s had.

"This is a dirty job," she commented.

"Someone's got to do it. The sooner we get this place in shape…"

She winced, even though he'd left the sentence dangling.

She still hadn't broken the news to Uncle Bren about selling the park. And, obviously, Matt still hadn't changed his mind about his ultimatum. But he'd given her sixty days. She had time to work everything out—starting right now with discovering just what was upsetting Matt.

"Everything okay?" she asked innocently.

"Fine."

"You and J.J. hit it off?"

"Yeah, we talked some last night and then again over breakfast. He seems like a bright kid."

"He is."

Still not meeting her eyes, he grabbed a long-handled broom and began sweeping up strips of peeled paint.

What had made such a difference in him from the night before, when he'd kissed her and walked off holding her hand? Something must have happened at his mother's house, according to J.J., but how could she ask about that? Not directly, judging by the scowl on Matt's face now.

She heard voices in the distance, the sounds of her volunteers setting up for work for the day. Who knew when she'd get a chance to talk privately again with Matt?

Crossing her fingers, she took the plunge. "J.J. told me you stopped by your mom's this morning. Was she surprised to see you?"

"You might say that," he replied sourly.

She looked at him.

He made a sound like a bull right before the charge. "I don't know who was more surprised—my mom or your uncle. What the hell was he doing over at her house so early in the morning?"

She felt a twinge of guilt. Why, she didn't know. She couldn't be held responsible for her uncle's actions.

Then why was she taking on the responsibility for what he had done? Why had she given up her dream yet again to save her family?

Why had she let herself believe in a *new* dream last night— one that could never come true? Her feelings about Matt were shaking her up, confusing her emotions, making her forget her priorities. She uncrossed her fingers. She didn't need luck right now, she needed a sledgehammer.

"How early could it have been?" she asked in a level tone. "You and J.J. didn't get here until eight. Did you go there before breakfast?"

"No, we stopped on the way over here."

Then it wasn't the middle of the night. Seeing the dark look on Matt's face, and already aware of how he felt about Uncle Bren, she knew better than to voice the thought.

"They probably have things to discuss about the park," she said soothingly, then could have kicked herself. Why hadn't she kept her mouth shut this time, too? Matt was too quick not to jump on her statement.

"What could they have to talk about?" he demanded, finally turning to look at her. "No one's seen your uncle around since you took over this…this project from him. It's as if he's washed his hands of the whole thing."

"I would think that would make you happy."

"Not if he's putting his washed hands—and his moves—on my mom instead," he muttered.

"Oh, Matt." She would have smiled, except she could see how genuinely upset he looked at the situation. There was something underlying his emotion about this; she was sure of it. "They're adults. I don't think we have any say in what they do."

He glowered.

"Or don't do," she added hastily. "You're jumping to conclusions."

"Is that right?" he demanded loudly.

"Matt," she protested, glancing over her shoulder. No one in listening distance yet. She'd have to be quick—and more blunt than she would ordinarily—if she wanted to finish this conversation before Matt's voice attracted everyone in the area. "What's wrong?" she demanded. "Why are you always so angry? Is it really all about my uncle, or is something else going on?"

He took a deep breath and opened his mouth to speak.

She held her breath—and her temper—and waited.

Matt had the uncomfortable sensation that he'd just taken the witness stand.

Kerry's uncle, with his conniving ways, was problem number one. But her probing questions had hit home. It wasn't just her uncle that had set him off. It was something more.

He stared at her.

She looked unblinkingly back at him, her head tilted a

little to one side, her brows arched and waiting. She wanted to know what was going on with him.

How willing was he to tell her the deep, dark secret he'd never shared with anyone? Not very willing.

Then again, he felt a connection with her he'd never felt with anyone. That became the deciding factor, the thought that pushed him over the edge.

"J.J.'s situation raises ghosts for me," he admitted finally.

She said nothing, but he could see understanding in her eyes.

He went on. "His story about Hector reminds me of growing up with my father. He wasn't abusive—at least, not physically. But he always got what he wanted."

"Controlling?" she asked quietly.

"Not even that." He frowned. "He made all the decisions but somehow made them seem they were *our* ideas, mine and Mom's. It sounds backward, I know, but it was as if we didn't have minds of our own. I was a kid, I could take it—I didn't even understand it back then. But it made Mom nuts."

"Which is why you're so protective of her now?" she murmured.

"Probably."

Who was he kidding? Definitely, the goal was to take care of her now. The softness in Kerry's face showed she realized that.

"Wanting to take care of someone isn't a bad thing, Matt."

"It is if you carry it to extremes."

"Yes, that's true. And it sounds like your father did."

"He sure as hell did." He wielded the broom furiously, not wanting to say the words that threatened to spill out of him. Not wanting to keep them in, either. Or maybe just no longer willing to deal with his demons on his own. "I don't want to be like him."

"You're not. Not the way you describe him."

"I've tried not to be. I've lived my life trying to help other people, not tear them down the way he did. Trying to build their independence, to keep them from getting into the kind of situation I lived with." He had to say the words. "But I could be like him. Maybe I *will* be." He tightened his grip on the broom. "Maybe I'm already recreating history."

"Is that what you're afraid of?" she asked softly.

"It's possible," he said, knowing if he didn't get it out now he might never make the admission. From all around them, he heard voices, shouts and laughter. The volunteers were ready to begin their day.

And he was ready to talk, to put everything in the open this one time. "I've run from it. Always. But the trouble with trying to outrun your past is that it takes you closer to your future. To your destiny."

"But that's not necessary. There's nothing for you to outrun. You're not your father."

"I'm my father's son."

"No. Your father's kind of behavior is learned, not an inherited trait. He learned how to manipulate people to get what he wanted. He chose to be that way. You have a choice not to."

He shook his head, but that did nothing to clear his confusion or send his fear away.

Kerry moved forward, putting herself in his line of vision. "You're a lawyer, Matt. Every time you go into court, aren't *you* trying to convince a judge or a jury to think a certain way? Aren't *you* trying to influence their decisions?"

He frowned in surprise. He'd never thought of it like that.

"You are like your father in a way, Matt. But in a *good* way. You're not using others against themselves to get what you want. You're helping your clients. Innocent people who deserve justice."

She'd nailed it with that, had put into words what he'd always wanted. What he'd always believed.

But he couldn't shake those other beliefs he'd grown up holding on to.

"What you're dealing with is not heredity, Matt. It's nature versus nurture, the man you *are* against the role model you were brought up with."

Her blue eyes had zeroed in on him as if she could convince him by the intensity of her stare alone.

"Take J.J. as an example," she insisted. "You don't know a tenth of what he's gone through. He's grown up with a series of men in his life, men who lived temporarily with his mother. They weren't all very nice—in fact, most of them weren't. You see J.J.'s black eye. I'm betting Hector's aim wasn't off at all. He *wanted* to hit J.J."

"That's inexcusable. But that's not the situation here." He didn't know why he protested when he'd already seen the parallels himself.

"It's a similar situation," she insisted. "My point is, as badly as those men in his life treated J.J., look at how he's turned out. Look at how he tries to make the right decisions."

"Joining up with a gang?" he asked skeptically.

"He made a mistake and corrected it. It's in his past now. That's what makes him better than a man like your father. That's what makes you a better man, too."

Unconvinced, he shook his head.

"We're not necessarily a product of our parents, Matt."

He looked away.

She put her hand over his. "Do you want to know how I know this?" She didn't wait for him to respond. "I've already told you my parents were archaeologists. Mom and Dad were in South America, on a dig that had already yielded some important new finds. They took a risk, a stupid risk because they were eager to move ahead without taking the right precautions. They didn't stop to analyze the setup or to think about the consequences. To realize that if something happened to them, they would be leaving five children behind."

Matt swallowed hard. Emotion laced her tone, but it was the unseeing look in her eyes that frightened him, that told him she was off at that dig, reliving something that had changed her world completely. That unseeing look made him forget his own worries, made him want only to console her.

"At that moment," she continued, "they didn't care about anything but the excitement of their excavation and their fabulous find. So they made a bad decision. The last of a series of bad decisions, over the years, including giving up responsibility for their own children. The decision they made that day at the excavation was final—and fatal."

After a long, unbroken silence, he murmured, "What happened?"

"They were killed in a cave-in," she said bluntly.

Finally, she came back to him. Her eyes focused in again, soft blue and sad now.

"The only thing that kept me going was telling myself I didn't have to follow in my parents' footsteps. And," she added gently, "neither do you. You're a *good* man, Matt. Don't be so rough on yourself."

Before he could say anything, she turned and walked away.

He swallowed hard, had to stop himself from calling out to her. From taking her into his arms.

Kerry had argued as passionately before him as he'd ever done in front of a jury. She was right in so many ways, it was as if she'd looked directly into his head and his heart.

The realization shook him, just as powerfully as hearing her story had done.

No wonder she had so much compassion for her family, her students. And him.

No wonder he'd opened up to her completely.

That realization didn't shake him—it scared the hell out of him. Letting down his guard could prove deadly to all the plans he had for his life, all the things he believed in.

But how would he ever find the strength to put that guard back in place?

"WE'VE DONE A HELLUVA day's work here, Kerry," Albie Gardner announced, rocking back on his heels and beaming at her.

"We have," she agreed, smiling and looking around at the volunteers nearly filling that end of the pier.

All day, she had tried to focus on her responsibilities, on overseeing her workforce, on keeping an eye on her wayward brothers. J.J., a tremendous help, needed no supervision and had already become a well-liked member of the team.

But throughout the day, all she could seem to do was think about Matt.

They were together, yet not together as she watched over the major painting project that had gotten underway that morning. Somehow, their paths never seemed to intersect. She'd seen him only from a distance. Even now, as the entire crew gathered for their end-of-day wrap-up, he kept himself apart from the rest of the crowd.

Apart from her.

The thought crossed her mind that he was avoiding her out of embarrassment for sharing his story with her that morning. She could understand that; she'd felt the same after telling him about her mom and dad.

Uncle Bren waved at her and grinned. He had shown up this morning, with Olivia on his arm, to help paint.

That probably explained Matt's behavior.

While Albie gathered everyone near the game booths, she stared down at her clipboard.

After hearing Matt's story, she realized the source of his anger about Uncle Bren's unreliability, understood his unyielding attitude over the amusement park restoration. Seeing him in this new light made her appreciate him more than she had already.

Not that it would get her anywhere.

Matt's feelings about her family made it useless to hope for a relationship with him.

Taking a deep breath, she looked up at the group assembled around her. "All right," she announced, "let's make this short and sweet and go home after a great day's work. Your effort was outstanding and our progress is phenomenal."

"We've got a great boss," someone called out.

Applause broke out. She waited for it to die down. Her smile wavered as she saw Matt with his hands shoved in his pockets. He leaned against the entrance post as if ready for a quick getaway.

She swallowed hard and looked down at her clipboard, scanning a nonexistent report. "Carl has given all the rides an okay on the mechanical end of things," she told them. The news had come as a very pleasant—and welcome—surprise to her. "They just need some greasing up and fine-tuning, and he said they should be ready to run."

"So, it won't be that long before we're operational," Albie said smugly.

Kerry held up a warning hand. "We have a way to go before we can say that. We'll need an official okay on the rides. Most of the rest of the repairs are cosmetic, but they'll still require a lot of work." She paused and waited for heads to nod in understanding. "Any areas with curtains or awnings will need new ones. Basically, anything made of fabric is rotted from age and will have to be replaced. So will the seats on all of the rides."

"Speaking of fabric," called out Alice, the volunteer from the Village's office, "what about costumes?"

Kerry frowned. She hadn't considered that. She looked down, making a note on her clipboard. Where they would get the money for all this, she didn't want to think about.

"Do we really need costumes?" she asked.

"Sure we do. The place wouldn't be the same without them." Alice smiled broadly. "But don't worry, Kerry. I've got a lot of years and then some as a seamstress. I can whip up costumes, any theme you'd like, quicker than you can blink."

"I hope your services come cheap," Kerry said with a wry smile. "But we're still going to have to reach out for a lot of donations."

From a distance, she could see Matt looking at her, his face carefully neutral. Her heart thumped hollowly. He didn't care about the financial problems.

She looked back at her volunteers. "Maybe we can barter with local businesses, get them to offer cash and products in exchange for advertising."

"Well, you know I can take care of that job," Uncle Bren said confidently.

That *was* one thing he could manage with ease. He had the gift of gab, for sure. She nodded at him—and didn't dare look at Matt.

Fortunately, her suggestion had met with a flurry of responses, which demanded her attention. The shouts came so quickly she couldn't write fast enough.

"My grandson has a real estate office," Carl told them. "He's always looking for promotional opportunities."

"I was in advertising," a small dark-haired woman said.

"I still know the manager at the copy shop. I'll get us a great discount on press releases and flyers."

"My boy and his wife own the fabric store," Albie said. "If they don't offer up some materials, I'll write them out of my will."

Everyone laughed.

Everyone except Matt. He had shifted against the post, half turning his back to the crowd.

She sighed inwardly and raised her hand. "Hold up," she begged. "How about, tonight you make lists of whatever ideas you come up with and turn them in to me tomorrow morning? I'll organize the suggestions, then we'll decide what we're going after and how we're going to get it."

"Sounds good," Carl said.

Others nodded.

"All right, then." Kerry put down her clipboard. "Thanks, everyone. And thank you all again for the great job you're doing, today and every day."

"No problem, Kerry," Alice said. "We've got a vested interest in the place, too, you know."

"More than that, we've got history." Albie smiled. "Why, I met my Louise here. She was the prettiest gal in the whole place. She worked the ringtoss, and I spent half my paycheck on it just so's I could hang around her."

"This pier's the best place in town for spoonin'," a silver-haired man added with a wink.

Knowing chuckles followed that remark. All of a sudden, the people around her had begun to look dreamy-eyed—and years younger.

"I worked here every summer during high school," Carl said.

"Me, too," said a frail-looking woman who had wielded a paintbrush with a vengeance that afternoon. "And it was funny, even after I got off work, I didn't want to leave."

"This place is magical," someone else said.

"Sure and y'know, it is," Uncle Bren shouted. "That's why it's called Rainbow's End. All the magic happens here."

He and Gran and Olivia Lawrence, standing on either side of him, sported a trio of grins.

All around, heads nodded and people murmured agreement.

She looked toward the entrance again. Matt was gone.

Her heart sank.

He didn't want the amusement park to succeed. He wanted it sold. And for good reason, she had to admit. She didn't like the thought, either, of any of the residents suffering financially because of what her uncle had done. What were the chances the residents could make a profit here?

But Uncle Bren and Gran were so excited about a potential success, she couldn't bear to see them hurt. And the volunteers seemed more than satisfied with their ownership of the park.

Restoring Rainbow's End had become a pot of gold for them all—a treasure trove of good memories. A way of rediscovering their youth.

How could she take that away from them? Why would she?

Maybe her family and their schemes weren't always as crazy as she had thought.

She looked around, seeing happiness and contentment tangible enough to display on canvas, and finally understood Uncle Bren *had* been on to a good thing, all along.

Suddenly, she realized she wanted the park to succeed, too.

But…

Helping her family would hurt Matt and his need to take care of his mother.

Helping Matt would hurt her family and all of these people for whom Rainbow's End meant so much.

There was no happy solution to this problem.

There was no answer at all.

Chapter Fourteen

Matt strode behind the game booths, trying to contain his irritation over this talk about the past and this magical place at the end of the rainbow. He blamed all the volunteers' misguided ideas on one man.

He'd already hired a detective to do a background check on Brendan MacBride. It was too late to cancel the job even if he wanted to.

And he didn't want to.

The money for the amusement park might have been accounted for, but MacBride still carried the responsibility for getting his mother and the others mixed up in a bad business deal. They could lose everything, thanks to him. He wasn't off the hook. Not by a long shot.

Especially not after Matt had found him at his mom's this morning.

His contact would have gathered the info Matt wanted by now. He leaned against the back of a booth, punched the detective's number into his cell phone and waited impatiently for an answer.

When he got one and said hello, Al responded promptly, "No arrests, no records, no complaints against him."

Matt frowned.

"He came up in a few reports, mostly real estate and financial transactions."

"Is that right?" Possibly something he could get a handle on there.

"Everything's legit, though," Al added, dampening his enthusiasm. "His personal financial record's clean. He has no mortgage."

"Credit rating?"

"Nothing doing with that, and he's got no major outstanding bills. He made some hefty purchases recently, but everything's been paid in full."

Thanks to the Lakeside residents.

Matt had to unclench his jaw before he could speak again. "Okay, let me know if anything does turn up. Thanks."

Stabbing the button to disconnect the call, he stared down at the water gently lapping against the pier. He couldn't see anything wrong with the pilings, didn't notice any damage to the wooden walkway in the area around him.

"Steady as they make them," that structural engineer, Carl, had said.

Matt ground his teeth together again.

He'd dedicated his life to fighting for strangers. And now, when it came to his own mother, he was helpless against the situation. It angered him to think Brendan MacBride was going to get away with this.

But he wasn't, if Matt had any say in it.

The deal was done, the participants in agreement about the renovations. Instead, they ought to be enjoying their money or reaping the benefits of earned income, not risking their financial stability on this investment. Not working themselves to death doing the physical labor running an amusement park would demand. What they considered a fun venture could have serious ramifications. If anything on the pier would prove the inadvisability of this entire idea, he would find it.

He had to.

WHEN THE LAST OF THE volunteers had gone, Kerry, with J.J.'s help, finished straightening up inside the shed. As she snapped the padlock closed, a loud metallic crash sounded from somewhere close by. She started, then turned to J.J. "Well, I know it's not you. But what *was* that?"

He shook his head.

A thin, high scream filled the air. After a quick, wide-eyed glance at each other, they took off running.

To her shock, when they rounded the corner of the shed, Matt was far ahead of them.

"Matt," she yelled. "Where?"

"Near the roller coaster," he called over his shoulder.

He disappeared from view. She was no match for J.J.'s long legs, and he soon outdistanced her, too.

She raced along, straining to catch up, praying that no one had been hurt. When she made the turn around the last of the concession stands and came into full view of the roller coaster, she nearly crashed into J.J.

When she looked up, her legs almost went out from under her.

Colin was dangling, face out, from one of the highest points of the roller coaster's framework, his legs swinging wildly as he tried to find a foothold on the metal bars behind him. Only the thin material of his T-shirt—caught on some protrusion that yanked the shirt tightly beneath his arms—stopped him from falling to the pier far below.

"Oh, no," she breathed.

Matt had already climbed halfway to the top of the structure.

Brody stood openmouthed staring up at Colin. She ran over to him and grabbed his shoulder. "What happened, Brody? What were you doing?"

He shrugged, scuffing his toe against the wooden plank beneath his foot. "Nothin'."

"Brody!"

He glanced at her, his eyes suspiciously bright. "We were only playing, Ker. Colin wanted to see how far up he could get."

He looked again at the roller coaster. She turned her eyes that way, too.

Matt climbed the metal frame hand over fist, moving faster than she thought possible, but he still had several yards to go to reach Colin.

A second later, Matt's foot slipped.

For a long moment he dangled as precariously as Colin, clinging on to the ride's framework only by his hands. Brody and J.J. cried out. Kerry swallowed a shriek and clutched Brody's shoulder so tightly she felt him cringe in pain.

Matt's feet scrabbled against the frame.

What felt like a lifetime later, he regained first one toehold, then another. Immediately, he continued his climb.

She loosened her grip and said a silent prayer.

Let Matt get to the top of the roller coaster in time. Let Colin's shirt hold tight. Let both of them make it safely back down to the ground.

And then she'd tear Colin to pieces!

"He's almost there," J.J. murmured.

She reached out and gripped his shoulder, too, as if holding onto the boys would steady them all. Or maybe steady the wooden planks beneath them. A lot of good that would do if either Matt or Colin—

She wouldn't think about it.

"It's all right," J.J. said in a hushed tone.

"Yeah?" Brody asked, his voice cracking. "You sure, J.J.?"

"Yeah. Mr. Lawrence's got him."

She held her breath as Matt lifted Colin with one arm, high

enough to release pressure on the T-shirt and long enough for Colin to flip around and grab the roller coaster's frame.

She could see Matt struggling one-handed to free the T-shirt fabric from whatever piece of metal had snagged it.

Long moments later, the shirt fell loosely back into place on Colin, and Matt looked down to give them a reassuring wave.

She sagged, her legs almost buckling again, this time in relief. Brody and J.J. each wrapped an arm around her. She held on to them, too, her unblinking gaze on Matt and Colin. They still had a long way to go to get to the ground again.

When Matt's eyes met hers, she gave him a return wave and the most reassuring smile she could muster.

He started the descent first, keeping close to Colin.

She swallowed a gasp, not wanting to startle Brody or J.J. Matt was using himself as a shield, a safeguard, in case Colin fell.

Her eyes suddenly filled and flowed over. She was too overwhelmed even to let go of the boys to wipe her tears away.

A long while later, Matt and Colin finally touched their feet to the pier again.

Brody and J.J. rushed forward to punch Colin lightly on the arms and slap high-fives with Matt.

"Colin, you jerk," Brody teased, "you weren't supposed to get caught like a fish on a hook."

"What were you thinking, anyhow," J.J. put in, "climbing way up there?"

"Don't even ask," Colin said. "It was a stupid idea, all right?"

"Yeah, Colin. But," Brody added in a stage whisper, "it was lots better than falling off the pier."

Shaking her head, she moved toward them, then stumbled to a halt, unable to walk as emotions shuddered through her.

Relief that Colin and Matt had climbed down safely. Fear that, next time, Colin or Brody might not be lucky enough to have someone like Matt around when they pulled one of their stunts. And anger—a terrible, gut-wrenching rage—at the idea that yet another member of her family had done something so senseless. So crazy.

So dangerous that she might have lost Matt, too.

One sob escaped her before she ran to Colin. She would yell at him—oh, yes, she would yell at him and tell him what she thought of his insane idea and punish him for the rest of the summer. But not now.

Now, she only wanted to hold him. She did just that, wrapping her arms around him hard enough to make him struggle for breath.

To her surprise, he hugged her, too—for all of three seconds before rearing back and pulling himself away. But she'd felt him trembling and knew how frightened he'd been.

"You," she said, her voice breaking. "Home. Now."

Eyes downcast, he nodded.

The three boys moved ahead of her along the pier.

Taking a deep, shaky breath, she turned to Matt, who stood at her side. "Thank you," she whispered.

"Nothing to it," he said softly. "With those kids, it's all in a day's work around here." With one hand, he thumbed away the remnants of her tears. "Come on, it's over now." He smiled wryly. "But we'd better keep up with them. I don't trust those two for a minute."

She nodded. "You've got a point," she admitted, and despite her effort to speak normally, her voice cracked again.

Walking along beside him, following the boys, she couldn't resist looking from the corner of her eye at Matt.

He was a good man. A wonderful man.

He was her hero.

But, of course, she'd known that all along.

MATT LOOKED AT THE clock on the dashboard. Right on time to pick up his mom to take her to dinner.

He left the Jeep in the visitors' parking area and headed down the street to her apartment house, still thinking about the day behind him.

Kerry had made some valid points that morning, when he'd finally unloaded a lot of his frustration. Her reasoning had started him thinking in a different direction.

Then her brother had pulled that reckless stunt a short while ago, and she had looked at him as if he were some kind of superman—making her as crazy as the rest of her clan.

He was no hero.

He needed to get away from Kerry. But first, he had to come up with a way to get her out of his system.

When he climbed the stairs and walked down the hall, his mother's door opened. At first he thought she must have seen him from the window and come to greet him.

When he saw who stepped onto the front mat, he flipped his smile to a scowl.

MacBride.

The man slunk away in the opposite direction.

Matt would have followed, but his mom now stood in the doorway, waiting. He trailed her into the apartment.

"I see your friend made himself scarce again," he said abruptly.

She took a seat on her favorite wing chair and nodded. "Can you blame him, Matthew? The way you act whenever he's around is appalling. Not to mention, sweetheart, it's rude."

He frowned. "And he's the poster boy of politeness, Mom?"

"He can be."

He didn't like her smile. He paced, wondering what he

could say to convince her that the man was a louse, and at the same time keep from hurting her feelings.

The hell with it. He couldn't come up with anything.

Maybe his memories were too fresh from the conversation with Kerry that morning. But he couldn't hold back. He stopped in front of her. "Mom, I just don't get it. Wasn't Dad walking out bad enough? Why would you want to hook up with another loser?"

"Matthew, I'm surprised at you! Brendan is not a loser—and he's nothing like your father." Her lips tightened. She shook her head and sighed. "We need to talk."

Great. He'd gone from hero to...who knew what, in the space of an hour.

"First of all, about Brendan. You haven't given him much of a chance. He's a good man."

The statement echoed Kerry's words to him: *you're a good man, Matt.* He shook the memory away.

She raised her chin. "And he's a good friend of mine, Matthew. I don't know if we're going to 'hook up,' as you call it. We're taking things as they come, and they're working well. Except for you, sweetheart. Your attitude isn't helping any of us."

"I'm only trying to keep him from taking advantage of you."

"*I* only wish he would!" She giggled like a schoolgirl, and he stared at her. "Close your mouth, Matthew. I'm sorry, but that was an opening I couldn't resist." She looked at him, suddenly serious again. "I know what you're doing. What you've always done. And I've always loved you for it. But, second of all..." She stopped.

Matt looked warily at her. *Now what?*

"Matthew, please sit down. I have something to tell you."

The worst was about to come. Slowly, he took a seat on her too-small couch.

She looked as put-together as usual, with her hair short and chic, her nails painted, her jewelry matching her outfit. A mom anyone would be proud of.

He thought for a moment of Kerry and her brothers, who no longer had a mother.

Across from him, his mother folded her hands in her lap, sighed and stared at him.

"This is worse than waiting through jury deliberation," he told her. "Just let me have it."

She smiled slightly. She'd always been proud of his becoming a lawyer.

"I'm not quite sure why I've never discussed this with you before," she began. "I should have told you years ago."

He suddenly realized she was talking past, not present. That was a relief. She hadn't known MacBride "years ago."

Then what was she getting at?

She cleared her throat and tried again. "You were so young I suppose I thought you wouldn't have realized the difference either way. Or maybe I didn't want to burden you with knowledge you weren't old enough yet to handle. But your father didn't walk out on us."

What the hell?

He stiffened. Was she going to make excuses for his father, now, the way she did for MacBride?

He sat forward, putting his hands on his knees. "That's not true, Mom. He did leave us. I remember the day. I sat on the windowsill in the living room and watched him walk away with a suitcase in each hand and another two under each arm. He took everything he could manage, because he knew then he wasn't coming back. And he never did."

"No, he never came back," she said gently. "Because I didn't want him to. *He* didn't make the decision to leave. I made it for him."

"What?" He shook his head in confusion.

"It's true, Matthew."

"Why?"

"Do you have to ask, with the way he treated us? Or maybe you do. Maybe I did as good a job covering up for him as I'd hoped." She leaned forward to touch his arm. "Your father was not a good father, not a good husband, not a good influence for you to have around. I couldn't let you suffer for my mistake. I didn't want to suffer, either. So I had to do something. And I did." She sighed. "I'm sorry I never told you before. Maybe it would have made a difference."

The revelation left him speechless.

Thoughts bombarded him faster than he could process them.

Learning this years ago probably wouldn't have had any impact on what he thought about his father. Regardless of the details of his leaving, he was who he was, and that hadn't changed over the years. Matt knew that from the infrequent times the man showed up on his doorstep.

As to this news making a difference to everything else in his life…? Yeah. As in, changing everything he believed in. Changing the career he'd chosen. Changing the family he'd never had.

He'd always wanted the television-role-model family, with himself the hardworking husband taking care of his loving wife and well-scrubbed, well-behaved kids. Nothing at all like Kerry and her crazy clan.

The thought felt disloyal, making him wince.

He'd never found that family, anyhow, and probably never would. How did you trust letting someone into your life, when someone else close to you has walked out?

Been thrown out. He'd have to adjust his thinking on that.

Most of all, his mom's news had already changed what he thought about himself.

All along, he'd believed he was the strong one in their family, he was the protector, the savior. Yet, his mom hadn't needed his help. She had protected him.

The news still had him stunned. He stood and paced again.

He'd made a number of erroneous judgments in his life based on something that had never been true.

What mattered now was, what kind of faulty conclusions had he been coming to lately?

Chapter Fifteen

Hard at work unpacking inventory in the storage shed the next morning, Kerry heard the unmistakable sound of a boy's voice mimicking a helicopter. The sound came from nearby, and she tracked it to find Brody at the game booths.

"Brody, what are you doing out here?"

"Just getting in some landing practice."

"It's a ringtoss, not an airstrip." He skimmed a plastic pinwheel through the air, its blades spinning, and brought it to a sliding stop on the booth's flat counter.

"I *know* that," he said with exaggerated patience. "Tosses are boring."

"What happened to cleaning the seats on the Tilt-A-Whirl?"

"That's boring, too."

"But it's necessary."

Matt came around the corner in time to see Brody rolling his eyes. He looked from her to Brody and back again without saying a word. It was the first she'd seen of him since he'd rescued Colin the day before. If he didn't want to get involved with the boys again, she couldn't blame him.

"Do I have to go back, Kerry?" Brody whined.

"No, you don't have to. I thought you wanted to."

He shrugged. "It wasn't what I thought."

"A lot of things aren't what we think they'll be, Brody,"

Matt put in. His furrowed brows and unsmiling mouth made him look extraordinarily serious. "Life's full of surprises. Sometimes good, sometimes bad."

"Well, that job Kerry gave me is bad—real bad."

Matt's expression said his life was "real bad" at the moment, too. Had their talk yesterday morning affected him that much? Would he ever forgive all the things she'd said? She'd meant them, but she'd gotten her Irish up at hearing about his father and probably hadn't made her points as diplomatically as she should have.

"She said you didn't have to do it," Matt told Brody. "What would you rather do?"

"Help you?" He made it a question, as if afraid Matt would say no.

Instead, he nodded. "I think that could be arranged. I'm going to be greasing up the moving parts on the carousel."

"Fun! Colin and J.J. will help, too. Okay, Kerry?"

"Just make sure the grease goes where it's *supposed* to go," she warned. "You remember what I said to you and Colin last night, don't you?"

He nodded solemnly.

"Okay, then," she agreed.

"Yeah!" Brody ran in the direction of the carousel.

She sighed and shook her head. "I *did* give them a severe talking-to last night. And even threatened to keep them home from the potluck at the clubhouse tomorrow night. Whether that will work or not, I don't know. Are you sure you want to do this, Matt? That job could take the rest of the day."

"As sure as I am about anything around here," he said grimly. "At least it'll keep them out of your hair."

And put them into yours, she thought as he walked away.

J.J. would give him no trouble. But, even after disciplining Colin and Brody about yesterday's escapade, she had her doubts about how much they would tone down their less dangerous antics. Clowning around was in their blood.

She thought again about what Matt had said. His words implied he would be with the boys and she wouldn't. In other words, *she and Matt* would spend the day apart, too. Is that why he'd made the offer?

Maybe he looked so serious because he was thinking of the other night and regretting that he'd reached out to her. That he'd kissed her.

Was he sorry he'd ever met her?

In that case, the added exposure to the youngest members of the MacBride family today ought to take care of that. It just might make Matt Lawrence go away.

Which might be the best solution for everyone.

AT THE CAROUSEL, MATT soon discovered that the gift of gab ran to the youngest MacBrides, too. They'd barely let J.J. open his mouth before taking over the conversation. And the focus seemed to be on their big sister.

"She's good," Brody informed him, "except when it comes to rules."

"Strict?" Matt asked casually.

"*Oh, yeah.* She never bends the rules. Especially about what we have to eat."

"Yeah," Colin put in. "She's got a one-track mind when it comes to vegetables. I mean, just because we're Irish doesn't mean we have to eat everything in the world that's green, right?"

Matt bit the inside of his cheek to hold back a grin and suspected J.J. had to do the same. "I didn't notice her enforcing that at Bill's on Saturday."

"It's the only place we can eat what we want," Brody said.

"Then she does bend the rules sometimes."

"Ha!" Colin said. "Not very often, that's for sure."

"It sounds like Kerry pretty much raised you two." He knew the truth but felt curious about what the boys would say.

"Yeah," Brody said, "'cause me and Colin were born after her."

"Our mom and dad were never around," Colin explained. "Then Grandpa died, and Gran was getting up there. Kerry kind of took care of us when we were growing up."

Maybe he didn't know the truth, after all. Kerry had given most of the credit to Maeve.

"Especially Brody," Colin added, snickering. "She even changed his diapers."

Brody glared and threw a greasy rag at him. "She did not."

"Did so."

"Did not—and, anyway, at least she didn't have to tell off some kid who was beating me up in third grade, like she did for you."

"You don't know that."

"Yes, I do. I was there."

"Yeah, right." Colin slapped Brody lightly on the back of the head. "You don't know what you're talking about."

"I *was* there," Brody insisted to Matt. "She went off yelling at that kid. Whew! You don't *ever* want to get Kerry that mad at you."

"I can imagine," Matt said drily.

Over the boy's shoulder, J.J. nodded emphatically.

Matt could see a teenage Kerry hauling off and yelling at anyone who dared do anything against one of her brothers.

Hell, she was still defending her family. She'd hauled off and yelled at *him* for having anything to say against her uncle, hadn't she?

Despite his annoyance at that, he had to admire her loyalty.

Matt and the boys worked hard for the rest of the day— even Colin and Brody did their share. Finally, Matt wiped his hands clean and dropped the rag in a trash can. "All right, guys, that's about it. We're done for today."

"All *right*," Brody and Colin chorused.

"I recommend you both hit the shower."

They took off running.

J.J. lagged behind, sitting on the edge of the carousel to gather their supplies. "Told you Ms. MacBride was the best."

"So you did. Have you talked to her yet?"

He shook his head. "Haven't had the chance."

"I know. She's busy. But make the time, J.J.," he said quietly. "You've got valid reasons for not being sure about going on to school. You're looking at all the angles. And that's good. But sometimes people who've been around longer know how to work those angles."

"You heard Colin and Brody. She won't bend the rules."

"And she shouldn't. I'm not saying that, either. But there are options. Financial aid, work-study programs, other types of scholarships. She might be able to help you with your problem."

"I'll talk with her. You won't tell her first, will you?"

"No, I won't say anything, J.J. You told me in confidence."

"Yeah. Thanks, Mr. Lawrence."

When he held out a grease-stained hand, Matt reached for it.

He wondered when J.J. would tell Kerry about his predicament and what she would do about it. It seemed like the load of responsibility she carried never got any lighter.

To hear all three boys tell it, Kerry was a paragon. But could anyone be that good?

Maybe she was. Or maybe, like her brothers, she'd inherited her uncle's ability to smooth talk people into believing what she wanted them to believe.

The same ability his father had.

Even the thought of classifying Kerry with his father made him feel guilty. That guilt provided incontrovertible evidence he couldn't ignore about the truths he'd tried hard to deny, ever since he'd met her: anytime he came near Kerry, his guard slipped. His emotions—good and bad—ran away with themselves. His logical, orderly, well-planned life turned itself upside down.

He wouldn't let those things happen again. He was intelligent enough to control them—and strong enough to resist her.

And he knew just what to do to prove it.

KERRY MARCHED ALONG the pier, deliberately going in the opposite direction from the carousel. She needed to stay away from Matt. It seemed more and more that having him anywhere in her vicinity was enough to do strange things to her mind, her body and her heart.

Though she had learned they were more alike than she'd thought possible, she had to stop letting him get close to her.

She couldn't walk away from her family and let them fend for themselves.

Which made by-the-book, law-abiding Matt Lawrence the worst person in the world for her. The one man she shouldn't think about. The one man she *couldn't*…have feelings for.

She reached the largest building on the pier, a vast barnlike structure with wooden pocket doors. They'd had a problem with the electricity in here, and Carl still had his volunteers working on some of the rewiring. Now that they'd all left for the day, she'd grabbed her flashlight to make an inspection.

She slipped through a door left ajar and turned on her light. Eerie shadows climbed the walls and scuttled across the channel of water that snaked its way through the darkness. Cobwebs drooped from the rafters overhead.

Footsteps echoed behind her. She turned to find Matt standing in the doorway.

"Oh," she said. *Brilliant.* She hadn't seen him in hours, and that was the best she could do?

"I saw you come in here and wanted to let you know I recommended the boys go home to shower."

"Did they get a bit dirty?"

"Do pigs like to wallow?"

She laughed. It echoed, and she winced.

He looked around the space. "What did you call this the other day?"

"The tunnel of love," she replied.

"Yeah, right. *Haunted house* would describe things better." He chuckled, and the deep sound seemed to reverberate through the building—and through her. His face, half in darkness, made him a shadowy figure. Her heart skipped a beat.

"This place doesn't look like much," he remarked.

Getting a stranglehold on her clipboard, she said softly, "Matt, why are you so determined to find fault in everything you see here? Why won't you give anything a try?"

One side of his mouth quirked up. "You're wrong, there, Kerry Anne. There's something I'm willing to try." He moved closer, his eyes twinkling in the glow from her flashlight. He took the light, clicked it off and set it on a support beam in the wall near them. Now, he was even more shadowed. A mystery man, half dark, half light.

She realized she'd seen him that way all along.

A ruthless lawyer, out to get Uncle Bren.

And a good man, her hero, out to save the world.

He took the clipboard from her, placed it beside her flashlight and turned back. Her eyes adjusted slightly to the reduced light, aided by the sunshine that filtered through the space between the slightly open doors behind him. She saw the outline of his body, so much taller than hers, of his shoulders, so broad, and of his head, now tilted down toward her. He slipped one arm around her, not pulling her closer, just holding her, leaving the next step up to her.

Her mouth went dry. Her empty fingers tingled. She could step back, pull away. Or she could take advantage of what might be her last time with him.

She twined her shaking fingers in the folds of his shirt.

As he tilted his head still farther, she tipped her chin up. Their mouths bumped, brushed, then found each other in the gloom.

Only the two of them. Together.

Forget families. Responsibilities. Trouble.

Forget everything but Matt.

There was something freeing about kissing him in the almost complete darkness, as if being unable to see allowed her only to feel, to block out her inhibitions and to quiet all her fears.

He tightened his arm around her, trapping her hands. She flattened her fingers against his chest. His heart pounded beneath her palms. When she ran her hands upward, she felt the twin pulses in his neck. When she cupped her hands behind his head, fingers interlocking, he groaned against her mouth.

He grasped her upper arms and held her steady, at the same time taking a half step back. Their bodies parted, their mouths the last to break contact.

With a gasp, she came to her senses—though her jumbled emotions didn't make any sense at all.

"Think we're done here," Matt murmured.

I'm finished, for sure, she thought.

"I think you're right," she said.

She kept her eyes tightly closed, feeling a hot flush rushing through her, rising to her neck and cheeks. Kissing Matt again was the worst thing that could have happened.

No. That wasn't true. *Enjoying* kissing Matt again was the worst thing that could have happened.

Oh, but she *had* enjoyed it….

He cleared his throat. Loudly.

She opened her eyes, blinking in the light. It seemed brighter than before. The first time they'd kissed, she'd heard bells. Now she was seeing lights? The man was a hero, but surely he didn't have magical powers!

Suddenly, she smiled, recalling where they stood: Rainbow's End. What was it Uncle Bren had said?

All the magic happens here.

Then Matt turned, and she saw what had caused the additional brightness in the building. One of the heavy pocket doors had been pushed open. And outlined in the streaming sunlight stood her entire family, along with Matt's mom.

Uncle Bren had frozen in surprise, Colin was red-faced with embarrassment. Brody just rolled his eyes.

All this was bad enough, but it was the women's reactions that left Kerry floundering for words.

Gran and Olivia turned to each other, exchanged gleeful grins and smacked their palms together in a high-five.

Kerry stared, speechless.

As it turned out, no words were necessary.

The group proceeded to leave, with the boys trailing at the rear of the parade.

"Jeez, Col, did you see them?" Brody exclaimed, his words echoing in the cavernous space.

"Yeah," Colin replied in an injured tone. "And Kerry yells at *us* for fooling around?"

Chapter Sixteen

Matt returned to the motel room to find J.J. had left him enough hot water for a long, much-needed shower—although, after the kiss he and Kerry had shared in the tunnel of love, he probably should have turned up the cold water.

With that kiss, he thought he could get her out of his system. He'd only made the situation worse.

A while later, he headed to his mom's. On his way past the clubhouse, he spied Kerry sitting beside the lake, leaning against a fallen log, an expression of contentment on her face, her limbs loose and relaxed, her bare feet buried in the grass at the water's edge. A sketch pad rested on her knees.

He had never seen her this at ease since they'd met.

He wanted to know everything about Kerry Anne MacBride, from the inside out. Maybe finding she was merely human, and not a paragon at all, would be what he needed to shield himself from her.

She hadn't minded telling him about her family, at least the parts she was willing for him to know. From years of dealing with clients and witnesses, he could tell she was holding something back. He wanted to know what it was.

Winning her over, gaining her trust, would be a challenge. But that only made the idea more appealing.

He parked the Jeep and strode down the slope toward her, already forming his plan of attack. Getting past the facade to the real Kerry would mean tackling the situation on her terms. She liked serious discussion. So he'd take things slowly and seriously, first pique her interest, then draw her out.

She might have artistic talent on paper and canvas, but he was an artist in his own way, too. With words. When it came to interrogation, he knew every technique in existence—and had created a few new ones of his own.

He walked silently across the grass toward her. "Hey," he said. "Finally taking some time for yourself?"

"Yes."

"I can leave."

She looked down at the sketch pad in front of her. "No, that's okay. You can stay if you want."

He wanted.

He moved closer to her and lowered himself to the grass.

She continued working, the charcoal stick in her hand moving rapidly over the pad in broad strokes, sketching the scene before them. Her brow furrowed slightly as she looked up from the paper and then down again repeatedly.

He watched in fascination as fluid, curving lines turned into the rises and dips of the roller coaster. As strong, slashing lines formed the framework holding it up. And as quick, jagged lines became the grass growing untamed under the entire structure. Even in black charcoal on flat paper, the picture came to life.

"You're good," he said quietly.

"I'm quick, anyhow," she said, but he saw her lips curve.

"Art's important to you, isn't it?"

She looked down at the sketchbook and nodded.

"Have you always felt that way?"

"Ever since I discovered crayons."

He gestured toward the pier and Rainbow's End. "That project's cutting into your time, isn't it?"

"Yes," she said, not looking in that direction.

He wondered how much she resented having to take over for Bren. He wondered, with an accompanying stab of guilt, how much resentment she held for *him*. Wincing, he looked toward the lake for a moment, then said, "Where do you want to go with your art?"

For the first time since he'd joined her, she looked troubled. "I've always wanted to make it to the top."

"What will you do when you get there?"

"Endow student scholarships. And donate a lot of supplies to my school district."

"You really do care about those kids, don't you?"

"Of course. All of them. Especially, J.J. He's so *good*, Matt. I think he can make it, if he can find the strength to persevere through a lot of hardships and maybe a lot of sacrifices."

For the first time, she looked at him, her face relaxed, her mouth softened. "Thank you for everything you've said to him. He came to me a little while ago, and we've talked everything out. He's going to get a part-time job, with luck possibly an internship. And he'll go to school." She sighed in obvious relief. "We phoned his mother, too. She misses him. I think she's finally realizing J.J. means more to her than Hector does. I hope so, anyway."

"Good. That's the way it should be."

She nodded.

"Speaking of phone conversations, I couldn't help overhearing yours when we drove down from Chicago the other day." He wasn't about to mention the call he'd heard in the game room. *That* had been outright eavesdropping. "It sounded like you were giving up something else because of the park." He hoped his casual tone hid how much he wanted her to answer.

But she said nothing.

Know your enemies.... Only Kerry seemed less like an

enemy now, and more like…something he didn't want to think about.

"Want to talk it over?" he asked softly.

"That's all water under the pier now." She shrugged. "I'd been accepted for a fellowship. The summer in Europe, studying art. I turned it down." Her words were simple, her tone flat, but he knew a huge amount of emotion had to be churning inside her.

"You couldn't have gone later?"

She shook her head. "It wouldn't have been fair to keep the fellowship from another student who could make full use of it. Besides, I couldn't have gone at all. Not with the situation here. I couldn't leave my family."

"How did they take that?"

"They don't know." Rubbing her thumb on the edge of her sketch pad, she said in a low voice, "There's no reason to tell them. It's no different from any time before. When they need help, I'm here for them."

Guilt stabbed him again. She *had* to blame him for this.

"And then," she continued, "with J.J.'s arrival, it was just as well. We still have a lot to work out."

That didn't make him feel much better.

How could anyone be so selfless? By turning down her fellowship, Kerry was suffering hardships and making sacrifices, as she said J.J. would have to do—all because she wanted to take care of those close to her.

The same thing he wanted to do. But what had *he* sacrificed for it? A few vacation days? The good opinion of himself from the residents of Lakeside, because he'd chosen to throw his weight around? Coming on so hard really wasn't like him—except in the courtroom, of course, when necessary. But Albie and Carl and the other locals wouldn't know that. The MacBrides probably wouldn't give a nickel for his reputation. And Kerry…

Kerry would care. Kerry cared about everyone.

He looked at the sketch pad balanced in her lap.

"That's you," he said, pointing at the picture.

"What do you mean?"

"You're just like that scene. All curves on the outside, soft and gentle. But strong as steel on the inside, holding yourself and everyone else up."

She looked at the pad, then across to the pier. "And I suppose I'm as straggly as the grass under the whole thing."

"I wouldn't say that." He edged closer, forgetting his goal of interrogation, forgetting everything but Kerry sitting beside him. He took her free hand in his. "You're unruly, for sure." He touched one of her curls and grinned. "Obsessed, maybe. There are a lot of words that could describe you."

Her fingers stiffened for a second before she pulled her hand from his. She slipped the charcoal into a box.

"What's the matter?" he asked.

"Nothing. It's time for me to get home, that's all. I need to go grocery shopping to help Gran get what she needs for tomorrow's potluck."

"It's more than that," he said.

".It isn't. Look, I've got to go, Matt."

"Kerry." He put a hand on her arm. "You can't just walk off without telling me what I said that was so wrong."

She stilled, for a long moment not looking at him. Finally she took a deep breath and turned to him, her shoulders slumping. "It's not you, Matt. It's me."

"But why? What did I say to upset you?"

She sighed. "About…about my being obsessed. Sometimes I think I *am*—just as much as the rest of my family. Gran with her green bags and refusing to ride in a car. Brody with his juggling. Colin with his mountain-climbing. My older brothers are that way, too. One of them was crazy about this lake. He almost drowned here once, walking the bottom of it with a homemade snorkeling outfit. When that didn't pan out, he tried building his own oxygen tank."

"Did it work?"

"Of course not." She laughed suddenly. "But at least he's turned *his* obsession into something sensible. Not like my pie-in-the-sky dreams."

"Such as?"

"He works for a company that lays fiber-optic cable in the Pacific. He got what he wanted, after all."

"And you'll get what you want, too."

"A fellowship. Fame. Success."

"I don't think so. That's not your obsession, is it?"

She looked at him in surprise.

"I think *family's* your obsession, Kerry Anne. Your immediate family and your extended family, your students. Living, breathing people, in other words, not static works of art. You take care of a lot of people. And what's wrong with that? You told me wanting to take care of someone isn't a bad thing. Isn't that what you taught me, Ms. MacBride?"

"Yes," she answered slowly.

"And you meant it, didn't you? It sure sounded that way, anyhow."

"Yes, I meant it."

"And so do I. I've never been more serious." He smiled, sat back and waited.

It took a while, but finally, she gave him an answering smile.

He sat up, feeling an urge to cover those curved lips with his. To taste her and take her. And to prove he was worthy of her.

Damn.

Inches away from following through on the idea, he froze.

His grand plan hadn't worked after all; in fact, it had

backfired. He'd thought getting to know the real Kerry would help raise his guard again. Would prove she was nothing special, just another woman he had no time for in his life. He'd thought this conversation would break whatever magical spell she'd woven around him.

Instead, it had only left him more entangled. And more exposed.

When one line of attack fails, his former professor had said, *move in from a different angle.*

The problem was, he didn't have another angle.

But he needed to find one. *Fast.*

A SHORT WHILE LATER, Kerry and Matt ambled silently but together toward his Jeep in the parking area.

She was amazed by his understanding, touched by his obvious concern. And ready to take a chance with him. To risk a serious relationship, something she'd always wanted but would never before allow herself to have. Not after learning the hard way what happened when any man she had an interest in got close to her family!

But Matt had met most of the wacky clan—and he was still here. That *had* to mean something.

Something special.

She moved with a lighter step, feeling as if a huge boulder had been lifted from her shoulders.

"We'll finish up early at the pier tomorrow. For the potluck," she explained. "I'll tell Alice we'll come early and help set up."

Beside her, Matt stumbled but caught himself before she could reach out to him. He didn't respond.

She waited.

Finally, he said, "That won't work for me." He paused, then added, "I'm cutting short my vacation. I've got to get back to work."

"Oh." Again, she waited, looking out over the lake, skimming the length of the pier and Rainbow's End. When he still said nothing, she shifted her gaze back to him. "You hadn't mentioned that before. Something important came up?"

"You could say that."

She frowned. "But are *you* saying that?"

"Well…" He ran his thumbnail across his eyebrow. She'd seen him make that movement several times before, always when he was uncomfortable or at a loss for words.

She kept her eyes forward, watching where she walked. Anything but look at Matt. How foolish of her. She was now ready for commitment; he was poised for escape.

"I suppose I should be grateful that you won't lie to me outright," she said.

"I don't lie."

"And I don't play games. I told you that before." She sighed. "I'm a teacher, Matt. I recognize evasive answers when I hear them. What happened," she asked carefully, "about never being more serious?"

"I meant about you. We were talking about you."

"Okay…then what do we call the rest of that conversation we just had?" She shook her head sadly. "Did you think I didn't know you were trying to draw me out with your questions? I thought it was because you were interested. Now, I'm wondering if it was something else." She waited, received no response, moved on. "Maybe you saw the situation as an opportunity for you. A chance to practice your lawyer's interrogation tricks."

She waited again, her breath stilled but her mind racing.

Tell me I'm wrong, damn it. Tell me you meant what you'd said.

He remained quiet, not looking at her.

Her heart squeezed painfully. Her lungs struggled to take

in air. "You can't even deny it?" she asked, choking on the question.

He still refused to answer. Yet the muscles in his throat contracted strongly, and his shoulders grew more rigid.

Her heart squeezed again, but this time in sympathy for him. Obviously he was struggling, too.

"Matt, think about this. We're coming close to something, you know we are. Not that we've made any promises, but we're close to a relationship of *some* kind. I think you see that, and you're running away from the responsibility of it—just as you told me you've tried to run from your past."

He shifted slightly, turning from her. She could see the tension in his jaw. Much as she didn't want to upset him, she knew she had to go on.

"I'm not saying this just for me, Matt. I'm trying to help you."

"I don't need help."

The words were forced through clenched teeth. She could see the muscles working furiously in his neck. Her heart went out to him. "Matt, sometimes we don't know what we need until someone points it out to us, the way you did for me about my obsession. What kind of friend would I be—what kind of person—if I didn't return the favor?"

"And I don't need favors."

"You're getting this one anyway." She took a deep breath, raised one shaking hand, rested it on his arm. "It's like art. Sometimes, it's hard to know what we want to capture on canvas until we get a different perspective."

Lines formed around his eyes as he squinted, then he turned his head away. Still, he wouldn't speak to her.

Her heart broke, knowing what he must be going through, knowing from her own experience how difficult it was to deny a truth you've held your entire life. "Sometimes, it's also hard to realize the beliefs we've grown up with aren't real."

"Mine sure weren't." He stopped and looked at her.

She came to a halt. The harsh expression and the bitterness in his tone startled her, but she knew they weren't directed at her. "What do you mean?"

"My father." He laughed suddenly. "All along, I'd thought he was the one who walked out on us. Turns out, I was wrong. My mother kicked him out."

"How do you know?" she asked quietly.

"Mom."

A one-word answer that said he held back a lot more.

"I'm sorry, Matt. It seems your ideas are based on faulty assumptions, exactly the way mine were." She touched his arm. "But you see what that means? You don't need to keep running from any kind of commitment because you think that's what your father did and you're destined to do the same."

His arm jerked beneath her fingers, as if she had jolted him. Her eyes blurred with sympathy, but she knew she had to keep pushing, to help him understand himself the way he'd helped her.

"Your mother's a lot stronger person than you thought."

"Yes, I can see that now. And I'm glad."

"You're a strong person, too. You also don't need to keep running from the past because you didn't take care of her the way you thought you should." She tightened her fingers on his arm. "More important, you don't need redemption from ideas that were false to begin with."

He moved, pulling himself from her grasp.

She took a deep breath, knowing how deep Matt's beliefs went.

He'd handled the news about his mother well, had even sounded proud of her strength.

Would he ever be able to accept his father's weakness?

Or forgive her for pushing him like this?

Stiffening her spine, she stood tall, bracing herself for any response he might make. Ready for anything he might say.

Except for what he actually said.

Which was nothing.

Without uttering a word, without looking back, without hesitating at all, he simply walked away.

Chapter Seventeen

Kerry tossed and turned the entire night, getting no sleep at all. After picking listlessly at her breakfast, she left the house with the boys and headed to Rainbow's End.

They found J.J. leaning against the railing at the storage shed, waiting for them. When she unlocked the door, he waited for the younger boys to enter, then followed them all inside.

"Ms. MacBride," he mumbled, "Mr. Lawrence's gone."

Frowning, she turned to him. "What do you mean?"

"He left last night, after we ate. Left Lakeside, I mean. Said he had to get back for work."

"Oh." She tried a reassuring smile and wished she hadn't when she saw the expression in his eyes. She hadn't fooled him for an instant. "It's okay, J.J. He told me he was going back. I just didn't realize he was leaving that quickly."

She *did* realize one thing for sure, though—that she'd been a fool. For hoping the truth would help him, as it had helped her. And for believing a relationship between them would make him want to stop running.

"Hey," Colin said. "He can't leave. He never finished the work he was doing here, Kerry."

"Yes, I know."

"Want us to go bring him back?" Brody asked.

"Yeah," Colin added, sticking his chin out aggressively.

"We'll get him here again. We'll drag him back if we have to, kicking and screaming the whole way."

"Yeah," Brody agreed.

"Thank you," she said. "That's not necessary. But I do appreciate the offer."

The three boys simply stared at her.

"He'll probably be back in a few days, once he takes care of some things at work. Lawyers have busy schedules, you know."

None of them said anything.

"Well, what are all of you doing standing around?" she demanded, trying for a more genuine smile this time. "Now that we're a man short, we've all got more work to do."

"Yeah, that's right." Brody looked downcast but picked up a half-full paint can and a brush. "C'mon, you guys."

"I don't see why he had to go off and leave," Colin grumbled, but he followed suit. As the two boys headed out the door, he added, "How can he just walk off? He's supposed to be part of the team."

They went through the doorway.

Kerry clung tightly to her clipboard, knowing she was responsible for their losing a good worker. And for more than that.

J.J. drifted into her line of vision, his hands shoved in his pockets, one athletic shoe dragging on the unvarnished wood floor. He looked like a kid called to the principal's office.

"What is it, J.J.?"

"He's not coming back, Ms. MacBride."

The words she attempted caught in her throat. She looked away from him, swallowed hard, then looked back again. "What makes you say that?"

"He gave me money."

Her eyes widened.

"I didn't ask for it!" he protested.

He had jumped to a conclusion. How could she not recognize the reaction, when she'd done the same herself just the night before? She had only herself to blame for Matt's departure, because she'd made the mistake of letting herself get serious.

Because she'd jumped to a conclusion Matt had never intended.

And now, J.J. assumed she believed he'd asked Matt for money. "I'm sure he gave it to you because he wanted to, J.J."

"I told him I didn't need any, but he said he wanted me to have it. Guess he didn't want me to run short and have to ask you."

"That could be true. That was thoughtful of him. But it doesn't necessarily mean he's not coming back."

"Ms. MacBride." This time, J.J. looked away. "He stopped in the motel office last night, then he came back to the room and told me he was leaving. He said he paid for the room for the rest of the summer, so I wouldn't have to worry about it. He even gave me the receipt."

Her eyes suddenly burned with tears. She blinked them away, not wanting J.J. to see them.

But he stared at her, his own eyes hooded and his mouth down-turned as if he knew just what she was feeling. "I'm sorry, Ms. MacBride."

She nodded and sighed. "I'm sorry, too, J.J."

He turned and left the shack.

She wanted to hate Matt for what he had done. For quitting before the job was finished. For leaving them all behind.

For running away from her.

But she clutched the clipboard to her chest, remembering how carefully he had pulled it from her nerveless fingers just before the first time he had kissed her. He'd been so gentle then.

And so kind now, with what he had done to take care of J.J.

He had been such a good man and had shown so much compassion—and this, after she had accused him of being an opportunist.

That guilty knowledge made her feel even worse.

As soon as he'd gotten up the morning after his return to Chicago, Matt changed into his running gear and headed for the track. He wasn't expected at the office. He had nowhere else he had to be. And he hoped the physical exercise would burn up some of his nervous energy.

As usual, he stopped by Mary's kiosk with a to-go cup of tea. Somehow, even before he got to the track, he found himself running—running off at the mouth.

"Mom sure had the right idea in ditching the bum she once married."

"Guess you're talking about your father," Mary said.

"Yeah. If I have to call him that."

"You do, and that's probably why it bugs you so much. But is there something more going on?"

Matt put one foot forward, shifting his weight, stretching muscles in preparation for the furious sprint he would need to outrun his thoughts.

"Avoiding me, Mr. Lawrence?" Mary asked.

"No. Just the question."

"Or the answer?"

He laughed ruefully. "You never quit, do you, Mary?"

"Neither do you." She gave him her toothless grin.

"It occurred to me, finally, that Mom's got the right to invest her money any way she chooses."

"*Now* you're talking." She beamed. "What else?"

Frowning, he looked at her, feeling like a kid facing the teacher and having no clue about the answer to the question.

The scenario made him think of Kerry—precisely what he was trying to avoid. "What makes you think there's anything more?"

"Because you look like you swallowed your socks and don't much like the taste of them."

He laughed without humor. "You're zeroing in, aren't you?"

"As in…?"

"As in, what I *ought* to be swallowing."

"Yeah—and sometimes pride tastes worse than sweaty socks."

"It does." He switched legs, leaned forward, rested his elbow on his bent knee. "It also occurred to me that Mom might have picked a real winner with the amusement park— something that could turn out to be a good thing, after all."

"Hurts to admit that, huh?"

He shrugged. "As much as confessing anything else, I guess."

"So, I guess you got something to say to this Kerry girl?"

"I've already said it." He added sheepishly, "I went after her like she was a hostile witness."

"No surprise to me. You came on, no-holds-barred, same as in the courtroom. At exactly the wrong time for it, I'd bet."

He winced. "That was a low blow, Mary."

"Just telling it like it is. Okay, so you went around it the wrong way. Doesn't mean the verdict's in yet." She braced both hands on the kiosk's counter and leaned forward. "Didn't you once say to me cross-examination's where a good lawyer can make or break a case?"

Matt stared at her in surprise. "I believe I did, a long time ago. How could you have remembered that?"

"I *always* remember when a lawyer gives out free advice." She winked. "And I always make sure I return the favor."

THREE WEEKS LATER, FACING a long weekend alone, Matt brought an armload of work home from the office. Maybe that would distract him.

Late Saturday morning, he took another look at the file he'd spread open on his desk. It was the third attempt he'd made in as many hours, but he couldn't seem to concentrate. Every time he tried to focus on a page, Kerry's face swam into view.

She was right about his running. He'd taken off from the situation with her, trying to outrun the present the way he always outran the past.

What he should have done was stay there and wait for her to apologize for jumping to a conclusion he'd never intended— and then blaming her misunderstanding on him. He'd said nothing to her about a permanent arrangement. She had made a real leap in logic with that idea.

He had already put that entire last conversation out of his mind. But why, now that he was on his own again, did he have such trouble putting *her* out of his mind?

His mom's near-daily updates hadn't helped his mood at all.

The renovations were moving along at top speed.

The entire town of Lakeside seemed to want in on the action at the amusement park.

And even MacBride appeared to have redeemed himself. Donations from local merchants had flooded in—whether from Bren's persuasive abilities or because of the magic of Rainbow's End, Matt couldn't say. He hated to admit it, but probably a little of both.

Downstairs, the doorbell rang. He jumped up from his office chair, eager for any distraction. Right now, a political canvasser would be more welcome than his own thoughts.

As he headed down the stairs, the idea occurred to him that Kerry had realized her mistake, had come back to Chicago to tell him she was wrong about assuming they had a permanent relationship. To deliver her apology in person. The idea took hold so firmly that by the time he reached the door and yanked it open, he was smiling, knowing he'd find her on the front step.

Not quite.

Instead of the MacBride he expected to see, he found the male section of the clan standing in a clump outside, with J.J. hovering in the background. Brody and Colin stood so close to the door, they'd slipped through the opening before he could catch his breath and ask what the hell they were doing here.

"Why don't you all just come on in?" he asked, throwing the door open wider, not bothering to hide his frown.

"Don't mind if we do," Brendan MacBride said, not bothering to acknowledge Matt's expression.

Matt would have ground his teeth together in frustration, except that J.J. hung back, unsure of his welcome, and Matt didn't want the boy to think he was angry with him for showing up on his doorstep. Besides, he'd bet next month's billable hours Kerry's crazy relatives hadn't given him a say in the matter.

He waved J.J. inside, slammed the door and turned to face his guests, ready for the lynching he knew they planned to provide. Good to see the MacBride family had the slightest measure of the loyalty Kerry gave them. "Nice of you all to drop in. I suppose you happened to be in the neighborhood."

"Yes, indeed—" Bren began.

"Uh-uh," Brody blurted at the same time. "We drove up here special to see you."

Bren shot him a look but said nothing.

"Gran woulda come, too," Brody continued, "but you know she's got this thing about motors."

"Right." No mention of Kerry. Matt raised a brow. "And what can I do for you all?"

Bren smiled and let loose with a rush of words. "Well, first of all, lad, you can come back to Rainbow's End and finish what you started."

Matt stared, barely able to keep his jaw from dropping to the floor. "That's pretty good, coming from a—" He bit off the words, glanced at the boys, sent a crooked grin toward J.J., and finally looked back at the eldest MacBride present. "Coming from a man I haven't seen much of lately."

"I've been pulling donations together on this project, you know." Bren waved his hand, as if proof of his success would materialize at his command. "Working on things behind the scenes, let us say."

And behind everyone's back. He didn't voice the words.

He really *was* mellowing.

"It's like this, Mr. Lawrence," J.J. said, stepping forward. "We thought since you was so interested in the park and all, you might want to come back."

"Help with the grand opening," Bren added.

"Everything's almost finished," Brody said eagerly. "You should see that roller coaster run!"

"The tunnel of love's looking good, too." Colin stared at him in wide-eyed innocence.

Matt stared back. Whatever he might have said was cut off by the ringing of the doorbell.

Kerry.

About time.

Who knew what they would say to each other. Of course, he wouldn't have their discussion in front of this whole crew. Still, filled with anticipation, he yanked open the door again.

And again, he hadn't come close to guessing right about the person he'd find standing on his doorstep.

He opened his mouth and, conscious of the group in the living room behind him, snapped his jaw closed again. This latest development would make a hot situation volatile. Before he could step through the doorway, his hesitation blew up in his face.

"What's up, Matt? Aren't you going to invite your dear old dad in?"

HIS FATHER HAD AN uncanny knack of appearing on the rare Saturday Matt would be home catching up on work, rather than spending the day at his office. Usually, he wanted a handout or a free meal. The meal usually got Matt off easy.

Nothing could have convinced him to allow his father into the town house today. Instead, he waved the MacBrides outside, made rapid introductions, and walked them all down to the corner deli for a quick bite of lunch. Or so he'd planned.

His father had other ideas.

The deli didn't serve full meals, so they went to a steakhouse. The restaurant wasn't yet open for lunch, but his father took care of that. Then his dad decided the table they were offered was too close to the kitchen. By the time they'd settled into a spacious corner booth, Matt had lost his appetite.

He sat listening to his father and Bren trying to outtalk each other and watching as the boys all looked on.

"That one idea I had a few years ago, to modify all the local highway signs, just didn't work out," Bren was saying. He sighed. "Too bad. We could've helped all the off-the-beaten-track towns in the state a lot with that. Then I was taking the idea to Washington."

"Too global," Matt's father said, brushing the idea aside. "Too much chance for government interference in the profits. Now, that park sounds like a great venture." Matt could nearly see the dollar signs in his eyes. "Wish I had my checkbook here so I could drop a few thousand on you, MacBride, but I only carry credit cards." He shook his head. "I'm good for it, though—Matt'll vouch for me, won't you, boy? Hey, as a matter of fact, why don't you float me a loan so I can help these people out?"

"Sorry, I haven't got an extra dime." Matt stabbed his baked potato with the steak knife. "In fact," he added, "I wasn't expecting this fancy lunch. Since you've got the credit, how about springing for the bill?"

His father turned almost as white as the potato. Matt could see his mind working, like a witness calculating whether or not to lie under oath. Finally, his father muttered, "Stretched to the max on the cards right now, I'm afraid."

"Uh-huh." Matt shoved a piece of steak into his mouth to keep from saying anything else. *What a con.*

Abruptly, he stopped chewing.

That was it.

His father *was* a con artist. An opportunist. A man only out for himself. Matt had finally gotten that message.

But Bren...

Brendan MacBride wasn't anything like that. He never had been. Even that night at Bill's Griddle and Grill, when he'd acted like mayor of Lakeside, he'd simply been gregarious and friendly—and a big hit with the locals.

Kerry had been right about seeing things from a new perspective. Kerry was always right, it seemed.

She'd been on the mark about her uncle, too. He wasn't a crook or a con. A visionary, maybe. A dreamer, for sure. He was a man who wanted to help others, like Kerry did. A man with ideas as creative as Kerry's artwork.

And, most of all, with a good heart.

There seemed to be quite a few of those in the crazy MacBride clan.

Chapter Eighteen

Kerry looked around her, taking in the crowd, the colors, the laughter and shouts, the smell of popcorn in the air.

In the past two weeks, everything had come together for their grand opening. Today, all the volunteers had shown up early to man their stations, the boys had behaved reasonably well so far, and J.J. couldn't have offered more help if he'd taken over the running of the entire park himself.

Even Uncle Bren appeared at the designated time, decked out in a top hat and tails.

"He's a fine figure, isn't he, Kerry Anne?" Gran asked, looking on proudly as he promenaded down the center of the pier, Olivia on his arm.

"That he is," she agreed.

"Olivia thinks so, too."

"I'd say you're right about that."

"A shame that boy of hers didn't come back for the celebration." Gran looked at her from under her eyelashes.

Kerry kept her mouth shut. In the month since Matt had left, she'd heard a lot of comments like that from Gran. And from everyone else. She tried not to think of him, and managed well—for all of five minutes every hour.

No matter which way she responded now—either by condemning Matt or making excuses for him—she would lose in the conversation. She simply smiled, waved farewell to Gran and continued along the pier.

At the shooting range, Brody offered a demonstration of his skill to anyone who would stop and watch him. He seemed not to notice the small group of boys who stood waiting to take their turns. When he finally looked her way, she raised her brows to hairline level and tilted her head so emphatically, she would have sworn she'd heard a vertebrae crack. He nodded, looking crestfallen, and turned to accept the boys' tickets.

Shaking her head, she walked away.

At the ringtoss, she found Colin surrounded by teenage girls. A couple of them seemed to have gotten the hang of the game and squealed with delight when they each hit their target. The rest were more interested in flirting with Colin. They halfheartedly flung their plastic rings toward the bottles then whirled to face him, as if he might have disappeared during the millisecond of time their gazes had been diverted.

She winked at Colin, who grinned back at her. The girls now pivoted in her direction. When she gave them a cheerful wave, they glowered as if she were their stiffest competition and then edged closer to Colin.

Stifling a laugh, she moved on.

RAINBOW'S END OVERFLOWED with people. Somehow, Matt wasn't a bit taken aback by the sight.

He worked his way through the throng, searching for a feisty redhead with a crooked-tooth smile. And, when he did find her, she'd probably come with bodyguards—all the MacBride males and J.J. with, no doubt, Maeve MacBride thrown in. He'd never get to talk to her alone in this crowd.

Then, to his amusement, he spotted a familiar face in an unfamiliar getup. Bren wore a top hat and tails and even sported a flower in his lapel. He looked like a cross between a magician and the ringleader at a circus.

He also appeared made for the part the amusement park owners had elected for him to play. He'd embellished the role with a heavy Irish brogue that seemed to hold the women, young and old alike, entranced.

For the first time since he'd met the guy, Matt actually found himself wanting to see Brendan MacBride. He stepped forward and succeeded in getting the older man's attention.

To his credit, Bren's wide grin looked genuine. He clapped Matt on the shoulder. "Welcome back, lad. Grand to see you here again."

"Thanks, Bren. Good to see you, too." And he meant it. He leaned closer and said, "Listen, I want to find Kerry and talk to her alone. I've got an idea, but I need your help."

Bren winked. "Well, if it's a tricky maneuver you're wanting, you know I'm just the man to get it done."

Matt laughed. "I'm counting on that."

KERRY MOVED TO ONE SIDE of the pier and stared into the water. Everyone was so pleased with the success they'd had in getting the amusement park up and running. So was she. She wanted that glow of happiness over their accomplishment to last.

Yet her happiness was dimmed by the knowledge that Matt had left, and by the memory of how they had parted. She had tried not to focus on that, had tried not to recall anything about Matt Lawrence. But other than the renovations at the park, it seemed all she could think about was Matt.

All she could envision was Matt.

Even a few minutes ago, she had sworn she'd seen him coming through the entrance to the park. But then, she'd been seeing him all day long—albeit in complete strangers, with the wide sweep of one man's shoulders or the toss of another one's head.

"Kerry, girl, I've been searching all over for you."

For once, she welcomed the sound of worry in Uncle Bren's voice. A nice, exciting, complicated problem that he couldn't handle and only she could—that was exactly what she needed to distract her.

No. To her amazement, she realized that was what she needed, *period*.

It suddenly occurred to her that she hadn't given a thought to her fellowship in weeks. Didn't care that she'd missed the trip to Europe. Wasn't sad about giving all of that up.

The truth of these realizations made her gasp in stunned surprise.

She belonged here, taking care of her family.

So she'd better get to it.

She hugged Uncle Bren and tried unsuccessfully to swallow her gleeful grin. "What's wrong?"

He frowned, looking puzzled, then hugged her back and said, "Big trouble. One of the customers at the Ferris wheel wants his money back, says the ride's not to his liking."

"What?" Well, she'd wanted a problem and now she had one. She grabbed his arm and hustled him into motion. "What's wrong with the wheel?"

"He won't say."

"He'll have to." She trotted faster, pulling him along with her. "We can't have someone making unfounded accusations about the park." Unfounded or not, any word of something wrong with one of the rides could be their downfall—a disaster for the park and the end of everyone's dreams. She couldn't let that happen.

They worked their way through the crowd on the pier and at last reached the Ferris wheel.

"Where is he, Uncle Bren?"

"I don't know. I left him right there by Carl."

A line of people waited at the gate in the fence surrounding the ride. Carl was busy accepting tickets, helping passengers into a swinging car, then advancing the wheel so the next group could climb aboard.

Kerry sidled up to him. "Carl," she murmured, "Uncle Bren said someone had a problem with the ride?"

"Yeah." Carl nodded. "He's still on, should be coming down with the next group or two."

She nodded grimly. "I'll wait and talk to him."

"Sure thing. Hang on a minute." He ushered a young girl and an older woman into their seats.

She stood back, watching as the next car swooped slowly toward the ground. A young couple alighted, and a grandmother and two small children took their place.

Yet another car moved downward and came to a rest.

When she saw its occupant, Kerry caught her breath.

Matt.

His hair was tousled by the wind, giving him a rakish look she'd never seen before. He looked at her without smiling. When Carl unhooked the safety bar, Matt stayed in his seat.

Her heart skipped a beat. Her legs turned to the consistency of the cotton candy being sold a few yards away.

"You're holding up traffic," Matt said.

She rolled her eyes. "Don't tell me. Let me guess. You've got friends in the traffic department, too."

He laughed and held out his hand.

She looked from Uncle Bren, grinning at her from the end of the long line still waiting to board, to Carl, standing at smiling attention beside her. Finally, she looked back at Matt.

Her heart skipped again. She would have teased him, let

him wonder whether she'd meet him halfway, if not for the touch of uncertainty suddenly shadowing his eyes.

When she took his hand, his warm fingers wrapped around hers. She put one foot on the floor of the car, and he helped her in beside him.

Immediately, Carl locked the safety bar and pushed the lever to sweep them upward. Kerry stared at the ground, unsure what to say, as their car advanced. After a while, she couldn't stand the suspense. "What are you doing here?"

"Getting into position."

She narrowed her eyes. "What exactly does that mean?"

He waved a hand and, as if by magic, their car floated to a stop at the very top of the Ferris wheel. And stayed there. "I wanted to get you alone."

A tiny shiver ran through her. "Why?"

"Because we need to talk."

"I thought we'd done that. Or at least, I had."

"That's the problem. You never allowed me time for cross-examination."

"What? I most certainly—"

"Shh." He rested his finger against her lips. "Please don't interrupt when I'm trying to apologize."

She clamped her jaw and stared at him.

He took her hands in his. "Kerry, I *am* sorry. I hope you'll be willing to hear me out." He glanced down, ran his thumb back and forth over her knuckles, squeezed her fingers. Then he looked up again. "So far, so good?"

"A B-minus. Maybe." She bit her lip to keep from smiling.

"You will listen, then? Even if we get off this wheel and go somewhere else to talk?"

Below them, a large group of people stared up at their motionless car. She nodded at Matt. "We'd better let them start this ride again before there's a riot."

He leaned over and waved to Carl and Uncle Bren.

Slowly, the wheel began to turn, sweeping nonstop full circle, bringing them to a rest at the platform on the ground.

People stared at them curiously as they alighted.

A small boy took his cotton candy away from his blue-stained mouth and muttered reproachfully, "Mama says it's not fair if you don't take turns."

"That's true, lad," Matt told him. "Sorry for holding you up."

Kerry swallowed a smile.

They moved toward the edge of the pier and one of the conveniently placed benches her volunteers had installed only the day before. The seat gave them an unobstructed view of the lake.

She stared out over the water, its surface brilliantly lit by the sun.

"Kerry," he began, "you were right—you *are* right—about moving forward and not getting stuck in what's happened before. About people setting their own destinies. I couldn't see that then, but I do see it now." He laughed. "Thanks to your Uncle Bren and the rest of your protectors."

She whipped her head in his direction. "What do you mean?"

"You didn't hear about their visit to me last week?"

"In Chicago?" Her voice squeaked in surprise. "You mean, Uncle Bren and the boys?"

He nodded. "And J.J."

"Oh, no." She exhaled heavily, feeling the rush of heat to her cheeks and knowing her face must be flaming. This was worse than Gran setting her up for a date! "So *that's* where they all disappeared to. I had no idea. I'm sorry."

"Don't be. Their actions show they care about you, just as you care about them. Besides, it might have taken me a lot longer to come to terms with things, if not for them and my father showing up."

"Your *father?*" She shook her head in amazement. "That must have been some party."

"It was. Only I wasn't in much of a partying mood and hadn't sent out any invitations."

"You mean they all just appeared on your doorstep? At the same time?"

"Almost." He laughed. "And as I say, it was a good thing. I learned a lot that day."

She raised her brows but said nothing.

"I learned the only real con artist at that party was the one I'm ashamed to admit I'm related to. But I've finally learned to let some things go."

"That sounds wonderful, Matt." She hesitated, but in the face of his admission, she couldn't be anything less than honest with him. "And it sounds like you were ahead of me. For a teacher, I still had a lot to learn. I only came to terms with the last of it this morning."

"What do you mean?"

"Well, first of all," she began slowly, "I'm not missing the trip to Europe a bit. I'd have loved going, of course, and maybe I will someday. On my own. But you were right. The fellowship isn't what's most important to me, isn't what's going to make me feel successful. My students will—they already have. I think I'm meant to be a teacher."

"I could have told you that. I could hear it in your voice and see it on your face every time you talked about any of your students."

Nodding, she said, "Then it's a good thing I've finally realized it, too. As for the second item I've come to terms with…" This wasn't easy to admit, even to herself, but she had to share it with Matt. "It hit me a few days ago that, deep down, through my entire life, I resented becoming the caretaker for my family. I believed I had no choice, that I'd been forced into it by circumstances. But now, I know that's not true."

"Let me guess. It's somehow connected to that I'll-handle-it-all attitude of yours."

She laughed. "Yes, in a way. I did feel a big sense of responsibility. I can't deny it. But now I know it was much more than that. You were right there, too—my family *is* my obsession, but in the best of ways. I took care of Colin and Brody and did what I could for my older brothers and Gran and Grandpa because I wanted to. Because I loved them."

"Isn't that the best reason of all?"

"Yes, it is." She looked away for a moment, then brought her gaze back to Matt's. "But I have to confess, when I'm away from here, in Chicago, I'm lost without them all. I probably let my students become my substitute family."

"Nothing wrong with that, is there? You're concerned about your kids at school, the way I'm concerned about my clients. In my job, I don't develop long-term relationships. But you often do. And your caring has an impact."

"I like to think so. My students are all special, in their own way."

"So is your family." He chuckled. "And I have to tell you, the MacBride clan still needs you, probably more than you realize."

She rolled her eyes.

"Don't brush it off, Kerry," he said earnestly. "It's one of the things I admire most about you, your strong sense of caring for your family. And I can see why. They're all good people."

"Even Uncle Bren?" she asked.

Matt had come a long way in these weeks away from her, had done a lot of thinking. Her family meant so much to her.

And, though he could hardly believe it, they'd come to mean something to him, too.

"Even Bren has his good points," he said honestly. "After all, he has to, if you care that much about him." He chuckled and tapped gently on the front of her shirt. "I think the heart inside here is big enough to take care of everyone. I only hope you'll allow one more in."

When she didn't say anything, he reached for her hand, felt it trembling, and closed his fingers around hers. "You said you felt lost without your family. Kerry, I've felt lost lately, too—without you. I know running off wasn't the right way to handle things. But I'm done running. I want to stay. Will you give me a chance?"

He suddenly found himself holding his breath, waiting for her reply.

His life, his plans and his future depended on it.

Tears welled up on her lower lids and threatened to spill over. She blinked them away. But she didn't speak.

His chest squeezed painfully. "I know you come as a package deal—and I wouldn't have it any other way. If that's what you're worrying about, don't. I'll do whatever it takes to get your family to accept me."

A long time seemed to pass.

From all around came the sounds of the amusement park—laughter and shouts near the booths, screams from the direction of the roller coaster, the music of the carousel. But there was only one thing he wanted to hear, and finally, at last, it came.

Kerry's voice, as she said seriously, "I told you once before, Matt, I don't play games." The words would have been cold and hard, except for the soft curve of her lips.

"No games, Kerry Anne MacBride," he vowed. "Just give me time, and I'll convince you of everything I've been saying. I'll win you over, and your family, too."

She shook her head and sighed in mock despair, even as she locked her fingers with his. "In that case," she said solemnly, "you'd better hope for the luck of the Irish—*and* the magic of Rainbow's End."

Epilogue

One year later

The lights on the pier at Rainbow's End lit a path to their favorite ride—the Ferris wheel. As their car swept upward, Kerry leaned back, snuggling into the familiar curve of Matt's arms and surveying the success story below.

All her volunteers had stayed on for the rest of that first summer. By the time she returned to Chicago for the new school year, she'd left behind an experienced crew. They closed the park during the coldest months but reopened it as soon as the weather turned warmer again.

Even J.J. had returned this summer to Lakeside immediately after his part-time job at college had ended.

J.J. had made the right decision about going to school, just as she had made the right decision about focusing on her students.

Tonight, they had all come together again to celebrate the one-year anniversary of the rebirth of Rainbow's End—as well as the six-month anniversary of the day she and Matt had married.

The car swept full circle, and they soared upward again.

In the bright moonlight and the even brighter lights lining the pier, they saw Uncle Bren below, waving his top hat to the crowd.

Matt chuckled. "Who knew he'd stick around this long?"

She smiled to herself. He and Bren had become friends— one of the many magical things that had happened during the year.

"He had a lot of incentive to settle down," she reminded him.

"Yeah." He shifted, turning her to face him. "Helped along by a lot of family interference. Especially from his favorite niece."

"His *only* niece." She smiled. "But you know that's not true. The signs were all there long before I arrived here. Uncle Bren and Olivia were a matched set from day one."

"Sounds like another couple I know."

"Oh?" she asked innocently. She waved her hand and, as if by magic, the Ferris wheel came to a halt, leaving their car at the very top, in their lucky place over the rainbow.

Matt grinned. "I love you, Kerry Anne. And this past year proves we were meant to be together. *With* your family."

"They *have* taken to you, haven't they?"

"Told you they would," he said smugly.

"How do you feel now you're married into that crazy clan?"

"You want to know the truth?" he asked in an astonished tone. "Like the luck of the Irish rubbed off on me."

She laughed. "Well, prepare to get even luckier, laddie. Remember that family you always wanted?"

"Kerry!" He grasped her hands and stared at her. "Do you mean—? Are you saying—? I mean, are you really—?"

She laughed. "I've never seen my smooth-talking lawyer so tongue-tied."

"I'll show you tongue-tied." Matt leaned forward and yelled down to the crowd. "Hey, people—we're having a baby!"

Gasps and shrieks sounded from below.

"Matt, you're as crazy as any MacBride!" Shaking her

head, she leaned forward. "Not right this minute!" she called. "Not for months yet, even."

"And definitely not soon enough for me," Matt said, wrapping his arms around her.

Now realizing there was no cause for alarm, the crowd below burst into applause.

And above the dark, still surface of the lake, fireworks exploded, brightening the sky over Rainbow's End with a thousand crackling stars.

* * * * *

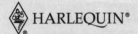

HARLEQUIN®

COMING NEXT MONTH

Available November 9, 2010

REQUEST YOUR FREE BOOKS!

2 FREE NOVELS PLUS 2 FREE GIFTS!

HARLEQUIN®

American ★ Romance®

Love, Home & Happiness!

YES! Please send me 2 FREE Harlequin® American Romance® novels and my 2 FREE gifts (gifts are worth about $10). After receiving them, if I don't wish to receive any more books, I can return the shipping statement marked "cancel." If I don't cancel, I will receive 4 brand-new novels every month and be billed just $4.24 per book in the U.S. or $4.99 per book in Canada. That's a saving of at least 15% off the cover price! It's quite a bargain! Shipping and handling is just 50¢ per book.* I understand that accepting the 2 free books and gifts places me under no obligation to buy anything. I can always return a shipment and cancel at any time. Even if I never buy another book from Harlequin, the two free books and gifts are mine to keep forever.

154/354 HDN E5LG

Name   (PLEASE PRINT)

Address   Apt. #

City   State/Prov.   Zip/Postal Code

Signature (if under 18, a parent or guardian must sign)

Mail to the **Harlequin Reader Service:**
IN U.S.A.: P.O. Box 1867, Buffalo, NY 14240-1867
IN CANADA: P.O. Box 609, Fort Erie, Ontario L2A 5X3

Not valid for current subscribers to Harlequin® American Romance® books.

Want to try two free books from another line?
Call 1-800-873-8635 or visit www.morefreebooks.com.

* Terms and prices subject to change without notice. Prices do not include applicable taxes. N.Y. residents add applicable sales tax. Canadian residents will be charged applicable provincial taxes and GST. Offer not valid in Quebec. This offer is limited to one order per household. All orders subject to approval. Credit or debit balances in a customer's account(s) may be offset by any other outstanding balance owed by or to the customer. Please allow 4 to 6 weeks for delivery. Offer available while quantities last.

Your Privacy: Harlequin is committed to protecting your privacy. Our Privacy Policy is available online at www.eHarlequin.com or upon request from the Reader Service. From time to time we make our lists of customers available to reputable third parties who may have a product or service of interest to you. If you would prefer we not share your name and address, please check here. ☐

Help us get it right—We strive for accurate, respectful and relevant communications. To clarify or modify your communication preferences, visit us at www.ReaderService.com/consumerchoice.

HARI0R

HARLEQUIN®

A Romance

FOR EVERY MOOD™

Spotlight on

Inspirational

Wholesome romances
that touch the heart and soul.

See the next page
to enjoy a sneak peek from
the Love Inspired® Suspense
inspirational series.

*See below for a sneak peek from
our inspirational line, Love Inspired® Suspense*

*Enjoy this heart-stopping excerpt from
RUNNING BLIND
by top author Shirlee McCoy,
available November 2010!*

**The mission trip to Mexico was supposed to be an
adventure. But the thrill turns sour when Jenna Dougherty
and her roommate Magdalena are kidnapped.**

"It's okay. I'm here to help." The voice was as deep as the
darkness, but Jenna Dougherty didn't believe the lie. She
could do nothing but lie still as hands slid down her arms,
felt the rope around her wrists.

"I'm going to use a knife to cut you free, Jenna. Hold
still."

The cold blade of a knife pressed close to her head before
her gag fell away.

"I—" she started, but her mouth was dry, and she could
do nothing but suck in air.

"Shhh. Whatever needs to be said can be said when
we're out of here." Nick spoke quietly, his hand gentle on
her cheek. There and gone as he sliced through the ropes on
her wrists and ankles.

He pulled her upright. "Come on. We may be on
borrowed time."

"I can't leave my friend," Jenna rasped out.

"There's no one here. Just us."

"She has to be here." Jenna took a step away.

"There's no one here. Let's go before that changes."

"It's dark. Maybe if we find a light…"

"What did you say?"

"We need to turn on the light. I can't leave until I know that—"

"What can you see, Jenna?"

"Nothing."

"No shadows? No light?"

"No."

"It's broad daylight. There's light spilling in from the window I climbed in through. You can't see it?"

She went cold at his words.

"I can't see anything."

"You've got a nasty bruise on your forehead. Maybe that has something to do with it." His fingers traced the tender flesh on her forehead.

"It doesn't matter *how* it happened. I'm blind!"

Can Nick help Jenna find her friend or will chasing this trail have Jenna running blindly again into danger?

Find out in RUNNING BLIND, available in November 2010 only from Love Inspired Suspense.

SHLISEXP1110